"When I was trying to shut that bomb down, all I could think of was you and Max Jr. I was terrified I'd never see you again, and I hadn't made things right between us. Then I walked outside, you were there and I thought, *This is my chance. I can do the right thing.*"

Allie crossed her arms and chewed her lip.

He recognized the defensive posture and pressed on before she shut him down. "I pulled away from you today because I realized that if the bomber sent that text, then he knew I was there and that I'd stopped his attack. Whether he was in the crowd or watching from another location, I couldn't be sure, but if he had eyes on the scene and saw you with me..." Max trailed off, unable to voice the unthinkable truth.

IMPACT ZONE

JULIE ANNE LINDSEY

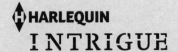

Special thanks and acknowledgment are given to
Julie Anne Lindsey for her contribution to
the Tactical Crime Division: Traverse City miniseries.

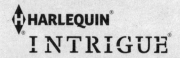

Recycling programs
for this product may
not exist in your area.

ISBN-13: 978-1-335-40146-5

Impact Zone

Copyright © 2020 by Harlequin Books S.A.

For questions and comments about the quality of this book,
please contact us at CustomerService@Harlequin.com.

Harlequin Enterprises ULC
22 Adelaide St. West, 40th Floor
Toronto, Ontario M5H 4E3, Canada
www.Harlequin.com

Printed in U.S.A.

Julie Anne Lindsey is an obsessive reader who was once torn between the love of her two favorite genres: toe-curling romance and chew-your-nails suspense. Now she gets to write both for Harlequin Intrigue. When she's not creating new worlds, Julie can be found carpooling her three kids around northeastern Ohio and plotting with her shamelessly enabling friends. Winner of the Daphne du Maurier Award for Excellence in Mystery/Suspense, Julie is a member of International Thriller Writers, Romance Writers of America and Sisters in Crime. Learn more about Julie and her books at julieannelindsey.com.

Books by Julie Anne Lindsey

Harlequin Intrigue

Impact Zone

Fortress Defense

Deadly Cover-Up
Missing in the Mountains
Marine Protector
Dangerous Knowledge

Garrett Valor

Shadow Point Deputy
Marked by the Marshal

Protectors of Cade County

Federal Agent Under Fire
The Sheriff's Secret

Visit the Author Profile page at Harlequin.com.

CAST OF CHARACTERS

Special Agent Max McRay—TCD explosives expert determined to stop a serial bomber in Grand Rapids, Michigan, before the detonations injure anyone else or put his ex-wife and toddler son in danger.

Allie McRay—Max's ex-wife and the mother of Max Jr., Allie is a small business owner, making baby clothes for sale at a local mall kiosk.

Max McRay Jr.—Toddler son of Max and Allie McRay, owner of their hearts, distributor of smiles.

Special Agent Axel Morrow—TCD supervisory agent, criminal profiler and negotiations specialist. Max's close friend.

Special Agent Selena Lopez—TCD K-9 handler. Surveillance, tracking and suspect apprehension expert.

Special Agent Aria Calletti—TCD team rookie. Narcotics expert.

Special Agent Dr. Carly Welsh—TCD poison expert.

Director Alana Suzuki—TCD director, fearless leader, tenacious fighter for justice.

Rihanna Clark—Former special agent, current TCD liaison for local PD, press and public affairs.

Opaline Lopez—TCD tech guru.

Fritz O'Lear—Grand Rapids bomber.

Prologue

"We're coming to you live from the scene of our city's second bombing in just three days," the tenacious female reporter declared. "I'm standing across the street from what remains of Burger Mania. As you can see, this popular twenty-four-hour fast-food restaurant was all but completely destroyed in the explosion early this morning. Police and bomb-squad officials are combing the wreckage now for clues as to who might've done this, and whether or not the culprit was also responsible for the bombing of a Grand Rapids real-estate office earlier this week."

The bomber coughed into his fist, covering a smile as the reporter rambled on. Law-enforcement officials wouldn't find a single clue about who'd made that bomb or the previous one. He'd taken great care to be certain of that. Officials would still waste their time looking, of course. They had to. But there was nothing to find.

From his place on the sidelines, he could see the big picture. The reporter couldn't. She could only see the loss of a building and a few lives. Same for her hapless viewers and the gaggle of lookie-loos gathering at his sides. They didn't understand the planning and precision that went into something like this. The sheer skill involved in what he'd done. They only saw the aftermath. The wreckage. They missed what truly mattered. The revenge.

Winter in Michigan is starting to heat up, he thought, chuckling internally at the joke.

The reporter twisted at her waist, wide brown eyes jerking between the camera in front of her and the rampant chaos behind. Her deep brown skin flushed slightly as the coroner's van trundled into position, joining the collection of emergency and first responders in the Burger Mania lot.

So there had been casualties. Just as he'd planned. Pride puffed his chest and satisfaction warmed his gut. He'd created the chaos and the carnage that made the pretty reporter shake in her high-heeled boots. If that wasn't power, then what was?

A gust of icy wind blew sleek black tendrils across her cheeks and against her glossy red lips. The scents of burning grease, hair and flesh seemed to fan her fear. "Five customers have been escorted from the building so far. Each was taken to a waiting ambulance, and most have already been rushed to local hospitals. Sources on scene are reporting three casualties, all Burger Mania night-shift employees," she said, her expression comically sad, as if she'd ever met any of those people. As if she'd ever graced a grease-mill like Burger Mania with her upscale, picture-perfect presence. "There's no word yet as to whether or not this week's two explosions are related," she said, "but you can count on us to keep you informed with up-to-the-minute details as they are released." She held her canned smile a few seconds longer, until the bright light on the camera dimmed, and the cameraman removed the device from his shoulder.

The microphone shook in her trembling grip as she passed it to him. She was right to be afraid. They all were.

The bomber lingered another moment, reveling in the panicked whispers around him. They had no idea how powerful he was. That he alone was responsible for the bombs destroying their comfortable little worlds. He smirked at the flimsy line of yellow plastic fluttering before him, nearly as pathetic as the ones who'd strung it. As if they could keep him back if he wanted to go. As if they could stop him from doing anything he wanted to do.

So far, he'd executed two perfect plans in three short days. He'd even taken a day in between to enjoy the news coverage and watch local police chase their tails.

He hoped his next victims were watching. He hoped they were afraid, too. Afraid to go to work. Afraid to leave their homes. Afraid because he could reach them anywhere. He was just that good.

The bomber watched a few more minutes, until the satisfaction began to slowly fade, and the grip of seething hatred returned. Then he walked away.

Fresh churning and burning in his core. Renewed anger begging for release.

Two down, he thought. *And two to go.*

Time to get back to work.

Chapter One

Tactical Crime Division director Alana Suzuki strode confidently from the elevator onto the seventh floor of the Traverse City, Michigan, FBI building. Her high heels clicked across the hard tile floor, her determination growing with each new step. The TCD would leave on assignment again today, and she never took their deployment lightly. The specialized unit of experts on everything from combat to poisons and hostage negotiation was infinitely capable and collectively unstoppable. But more than that, they were family.

"Good morning," Alana called, crossing into the oversize boardroom and making her way to the front.

The team was already in place around the massive table, tired eyes instantly on her. She didn't have to check her watch to know it was barely 5:00 a.m.

"Thank you all for coming in so early and on such little notice." Alana dragged her gaze over the fatigued faces before her, then rested it briefly on the giant FBI logo clinging to one wall. A sense of pride rolled up her spine. Pride for the Bureau. Pride for the thirty years she'd spent there. And pride for this team. "If you've seen the news, you can probably guess why you're here. There was a second bombing in Grand Rapids early this morning, and their local law enforcement could use our help."

The group exchanged silent glances, then turned their attention on Max.

Special Agent Max McRay had taken a seat at the front. Brows furrowed and hands folded on the table, he'd likely been there for a while. It was Max who'd woken Alana at half past two this morning, requesting she consider this assignment for their team, or send him alone if necessary. Max was an explosives expert, and there was a bomber in Grand Rapids. A city just two hours away by car and home to Max's ex-wife and toddler son.

"Grand Rapids detectives suspect a serial bomber," Alana continued, drawing the team's focus back to her. "After a long talk with their chief of police, I've agreed to send the TCD to their aid." She nodded to Opaline Lopez, the curvy, bleached-blonde tech guru seated at the back of the room.

Opaline lifted a small remote, and a big screen lowered from the ceiling behind Alana, images already appearing on the white backdrop.

"Thank you."

Opaline smiled, her brightly colored clothing and hair accessories never a match for her impossibly upbeat personality. She was a much-needed source of light on many dark days in their office, and one more thing Alana appreciated deeply.

"There have been two bombs detonated in three days," Alana said as photos of the carnage flipped across the screen. "Five people are dead in total. More are injured. The first bomb went off inside a small stand-alone real-estate office three days ago, at seven eighteen a.m. Two of the office's twelve employees were killed in the blast. A female office manager and a male real-estate agent. No one else was in the building. Official hours are nine to five."

Alana paused while the slide changed, then went on. "The second blast occurred at approximately two o'clock this morning. This time the target was Burger Mania, and the building was all but destroyed. Three were killed. Two employees in the kitchen and one behind the counter. A night manager and two staff members."

Selena Lopez lifted the pen from her mouth. "Similarities or connections among the casualties?" she asked. Selena was Opaline's younger sister and a K-9 handler. As the team's specialist in surveillance, tracking and suspect apprehension, she rarely missed a beat.

"None that we're aware of at this time. Two men and one woman at this location. All in their twenties," Alana answered.

Opaline changed the slide on-screen to one with candids of the deceased from both bombings.

Selena made a note on the paper before her. "Thank you."

Alana nodded. "Right now, local detectives and bomb-squad members have no leads, and the bombs are the only connections they've been able to make between the two attacks."

Max shifted, catching Alana's eye. "What links the bombs?"

The slide changed again, and Alana stepped aside, making sure everyone had a good view of the screen. Images of the aftermaths glowed in the dim room. The charred metal remains of the devices were showcased beside snapshots of the damage done in the immediate areas. A list of bomb contents according to a local lab formed a column beside the photos.

Alana folded her hands in front of her, giving her team time to take in the visuals before answering Max's question verbally. "Both bombs were homemade. Both used pressure cookers and materials available at local stores or online. Both were set off with a cell-phone detonator. The explosive in both was Tannerite."

Max's head bobbed slowly, knowingly. He swiveled in his chair to face his teammates. "Tannerite is a material designed for use in long-distance target practice. It creates a small explosion when the target is hit, sending up a puff of white smoke. The result saves the shooter a long walk to see if they landed the shot. If they're successful, there's smoke. Used incorrectly, as seen too often on YouTube—" he grimaced "—people lose limbs and lives."

Alana's gaze slid unbidden to Max's black dress pants. It was nearly impossible to tell, but Max had lost a leg, below the knee, to a similar device eight years ago in Afghanistan. Pressure-cooker bombs were widely used by rebel forces and militant groups there. Max's position in the bomb squad had put him in close proximity to dozens of such devices over the years. She'd recruited him for the TCD a year after the amputation, pulling him straight from the gym at Walter Reed National Military Medical Center before he could sign papers to reenlist. An army superior in her circle had given Max an unparalleled recommendation, and Alana wasn't in the business of letting opportunity pass her by. Max had intended to return to combat full-time, but she'd persuaded him to accept her challenge instead. Many civilian lives had been saved because of that decision. And he'd never let the loss of his limb or the prosthesis in its place slow him down.

"Tannerite is packed into a pressure cooker," Max continued. "It's surrounded with small metal objects meant to become projectiles and shrapnel. Nails and ball bearings, nuts, bolts and BBs are popular choices. A cell phone typically detonates the explosive. The pressure in the cooker amplifies the blast. These are rudimentary bombs with detailed instructions available online. Materials are inexpensive and easy to acquire. No skill is necessary for a successful build."

Axel Morrow leaned in across the table, anchoring his elbows. "So we're dealing with devices like the ones used in the Boston Marathon." Short blond hair and sharp green eyes gave Axel the stereotypical "boy next door" look. His easy smile spoke of mild manners and a wholesome upbringing, but looks were deceiving. At thirty-four, Axel was the team's supervisory agent, a fierce friend and formidable opponent.

"Exactly." Max nodded.

"And there was nothing unique left behind at the bombing sites?" Axel asked, swinging his attention back to Alana. As the team's criminal profiler, Axel was in his wheelhouse looking for patterns and clues in the details. "No calling card or other source of pride?"

"None," Alana answered.

"Is he targeting a specific neighborhood?" Axel asked. "Could these be locations of convenience? Maybe random sites near his home?"

"Possibly," Alana conceded, turning to examine the screen as Opaline changed the image once more. "The businesses aren't in close proximity to one another, but it's possible the bomber frequented the locations, making them familiar and emotionally comfortable."

A map of the city showed the bomb sites circled in red. Clearly several miles apart.

Opaline danced her fingers over her laptop's keyboard. "I'm sending you all everything I have so far. Photos, police reports, initial findings, witness accounts…"

Phones buzzed and chimed collectively before she'd finished speaking.

"Local law-enforcement officials weren't able to make any connections between the victims," she said. "The detonation days and times were different.

The casualties had no obvious commonalities in appearance. A basic surface review revealed nothing useful. I, on the other hand, hope to have plenty of leads for you by the time you reach your temporary headquarters in Grand Rapids later today."

"Which will be at the local police department." A familiar voice sprang through the open door a moment before Rihanna Clark entered. The former special agent and current TCD liaison for local PDs, press and the public smiled widely at the team. Her sleek black hair fell over her shoulders and her onyx eyes sparkled as she set a pair of stacked cup carriers on the table. "I thought you could all use a little help waking up. So I made a stop on my way in, while I worked out some details by phone with Grand Rapids PD."

The team went for the coffees, thanking Rihanna as they made their selections and returned to their seats. Dr. Carly Welsh, the TCD toxins expert, abstained, having brought her own large cup, as usual.

"TCD has access to a large conference room at the Grand Rapids PD for as long as we need it," Rihanna continued. "I've been assured the space is ours alone. We won't have to share or move for any reason, and we have access to anything within the department we might need. Personnel included. Their force is aware of what's going on, and they're highly motivated to protect their city and its citizens. As always, I'll be there to make any other arrangements you need. Just ask." She nodded at Alana, then took a seat near Opaline.

Alana nearly chuckled at the notion of anyone having to ask Rihanna for anything. She was a troubleshooting genius who anticipated the needs of her team with uncanny skill, then met those needs with precision and efficiency.

"Grand Rapids PD is expecting you this morning," Alana told her team. "Go home, make arrangements, then meet back here for departure. You know how to reach me if you need anything more."

Satisfied, and with a scheduled conference call in only a few moments, Alana excused herself from the room, confident the men and women of her TCD would get the job done.

MAX FLIPPED THROUGH the details Opaline had sent to his phone, grimacing at the senseless carnage. This wasn't the work of kids, drunks or idiots screwing around. Those kinds of people blew up old washing machines, microwaves or vehicles. This was someone who wanted to kill. Someone who intended to get the job done. Max pressed a palm to his knee, soothing the phantom pain several inches below the joint, where a prosthetic limb had long replaced his own calf and foot.

His insides tightened and ached at the memories. He'd thought for sure he'd die on that dirt road, a world away from home. And worse, he'd thought he'd gotten his team killed, as well. In reality, they'd all lived that day, though they hadn't all come home.

"Hey." Axel slid onto the seat beside him, delivering a cup of coffee Max hadn't been motivated to collect himself. He'd nearly finished a pot on his own before driving in today.

"You okay?" Axel asked, leaving the question open-ended. Allowing Max to decide what and how much to share.

"I've been better. I'm glad we've got the case, but I wish I could've talked Allie into leaving the city for a few days."

Axel pursed his lips. "No go, huh?"

"Not even close."

He bobbed his head in understanding. Axel had been around for the whirlwind romance Max had shared with Allie. And for the divorce that had followed less than two years later. He tapped his thumbs against the table. "Alana wants you to take the lead on this. Are you okay with that?"

Max dipped his chin. "No problem."

The rest of the team moved in closer, filling the space around Max's end of the giant table.

"Have you spoken to Allie?" Opaline asked, her voice thick with genuine concern.

The question earned her a hard, slashing glare from her sister Selena's eyes.

"I did," Max said, defusing the sibling tension as simply as he could. "She's aware of the bombings, but given there's no reason to suspect she's a target, she plans to go on with business as usual." Taking their son, Max Jr., along with her. All over town. To any number of places where a bomber could be setting up to kill another enemy.

Worse, she'd barely spoken with him when he'd

called. Max Jr. had been up, crying, teething, according to Allie, and she was in no mood for a directive from her ex-husband. So he planned to talk to her in person as soon as he got to Grand Rapids this morning. Hopefully, he'd have a better chance of changing her mind by light of day.

He rubbed his chest where a dull ached formed at the thought of his family as collateral damage. Max had already screwed up once, putting his job continually before them. Letting his desire to protect others take precedence over his duty to be present with his wife and son. He'd ignored Allie's warnings, and she wasn't one to wait long on someone else to make her happy. She'd left him and moved to Grand Rapids, where she could be with her parents and sister. They'd been there for her as she built her small company and raised their son. All while Max was off saving lives and preserving other families instead of his own.

The gonging silence turned his attention back to the team, now staring. Their expressions ranged from supportive and understanding to compassionate and clearly laced with pity.

"What do you make of what we have so far?" Aria Calletti asked, breaking the silence. Aria was the rookie on the team, a narcotics expert and an agent who'd earned his respect on her first TCD mission not long ago. She was young, beautiful and petite, not the package bad guys expected to find disguising a powerhouse. Folks underestimated her, and she knew it. She used that to her advantage often and well.

"I think this is about revenge," Max said. "The bomber's not blowing up old appliances to see if he can. He's blowing up people at work. He's not going for crowded marketplaces. He's not detonating at the busiest times of day. He isn't killing to kill. His goal isn't mass destruction. It's pointed. He wanted someone dead at each of these two locations and at those specific times. Times when the target would be one of the few people around."

Carly nodded at that, sipping gingerly from her home-brewed coffee. The tall blonde had been with TCD for three years and specialized in biochemical terrorism. Her honey hair and willowy stature reminded him of Allie, but Carly was guarded. His teammates all had a ghost or two in their pasts, something that kept them quiet at times, even mildly haunted. "Revenge," she said. "It's a powerful motive. And certain unstable individuals view bombings as loud and clear ways to assert their strength after feeling small or weak for too long."

Aria straightened, eyebrows high. "Well, all right. Let's go to Grand Rapids."

The team agreed and headed for the door. Pulling their lives together on the fly, well enough that they could leave for an indefinite amount of time, meant a serious hustle. Most were used to it. Max kept a well-equipped go bag that would carry him up to a week without having to call for laundry service.

He stretched out of his chair, eager to get on the

road. He'd requested this assignment, and even offered to take vacation time and go alone if Alana didn't think the situation required the entire TCD. He'd planned to show up at the Grand Rapids Police Department and beg them to let him consult. Thankfully, Alana had worked it out. Max was good on his own, but better with his team.

Axel sauntered along at Max's side. "You know, Allie and Max Jr. are going to be fine," he said. "We'll be there soon, and shut this bomber down before he ever sees us coming."

Max dared a look in his buddy's direction, wishing like hell he could will those words to be true. "You can't know that," he said. There were too many variables. Too many unknowns.

"Sure I can." Axel clapped Max on the back as they made their way to the elevator, smiling that trademark smile. "I know it's true because we've got you."

Chapter Two

Allie McRay motored through the crowded downtown parking lot in search of a decent space. Nothing too far from the mall doors or a lamppost. Winters in Michigan were frigid, and though it was daylight now, it would be dark before dinner this time of year. Allie needed to be prepared. She could blame her mother, the media or growing up as a woman for her intense fear of walking alone at night, but the real credit went to her ex-husband, Max, and all his horrific true stories of real women never seen again.

She shivered at the thought, then pressed the gas pedal a little harder. A minivan in the next aisle was exiting a prime spot below a security light. Allie's car slid in response to the acceleration, fishtailing slightly on a patch of ice as she made her way around the corner. Her knuckles ached as she gripped the steering wheel more tightly and cursed the freezing temperatures.

She trundled into the spot beneath the light, then shut down the engine and centered herself. Retail work in January was always a wild ride. Shoppers came out in droves to return ill-fitting and unwanted Christmas gifts. Many were less than pleasant about the exchanges, but that was the price of doing business. Thankfully, most people were thrilled with their Baby Threads purchases, and an upside to the January madness was the number of shoppers with newly acquired holiday cash ready to give her products a try.

Baby Threads was Allie's passion project, a small but mighty company she'd started at home so she could spend more time with her son, Max Jr. Now her custom-designed infant-and-toddler clothing business had its own kiosk at the mall.

She climbed out and hooked a series of bags over her shoulder. Her purse. Her laptop. A tote with more stock. Then she hurried inside, careful not to slip on any ice in the process.

The mall was warm and bustling as she made her way to the escalator. Scents of everything delicious wafted from the cafés and restaurants around the food court, making her wish she wasn't still committed to her New Year's resolution of making healthier choices. In other words, no more loading up on caffeine and sugar to keep her awake and peppy. This year she would rely on nutrition and exercise to help with those things. And only the occasional cinnamon roll, she reasoned. Because she wasn't Superwoman.

Allie made her way to the Baby Threads kiosk and opened it with a smile, thankful for the coveted space, if a little nervous about the bomber on the loose. She could thank her ex-husband for that fear, too.

He'd called her at three o'clock in the morning, upset about footage of a local bombing he'd seen on the news. She'd answered, barely able to hear his words over their screaming, teething son, whose poor little gums had kept him in misery for the past few days. She'd gotten the gist of Max's problem and request. He knew there was a bomber in her city, and Max wanted her to leave town until the man was apprehended. Not a wild idea, and certainly one she'd thought of many times this morning while she prepared Max Jr. for a day with her parents and herself for work. One bombing had been awful, two had been worrisome, and what she hadn't thought to tell Max last night was that she'd seen the most recent explosion. She'd run out for infant pain reliever when Max Jr.'s temperature had risen enough to make her fret. So she'd packed him into the car and headed to the local drugstore. He'd gotten a few blessed moments of sleep in his car seat, until the blast had woken him, and the emergency responders' sirens had kept him up. By the time Max had called, she was home and in survival mode. She could barely concentrate on anything other than her baby's cries, and she'd rushed Max off the phone.

In her sleep-deprived mommy mode last night, the whole experience had felt like a desperate blur, but as she'd gone through her morning routine, that had changed. She still wouldn't leave town. Being a single parent and the sole proprietor of a growing business meant she carried the bulk of responsibility for her little family's financial future. But she wanted to talk to Max again. Let him know she might've been a witness.

She rubbed chills from her arms as she set up her laptop and logged in to her inventory software. Memories of the blast and her ex-husband's pleas weighted her thoughts, but she couldn't let Max get into her head right now. Max Jr. was safe with her parents, and so far, the Grand Rapids bomber hadn't blown anything up during regular business hours. So there was nothing to worry about. She hoped.

Allie opened her tote bag and liberated the pile of new stock she'd brought from home. She put several items on display, then arranged older items on pegs and across the narrow countertop.

Today would be a good day, she decided. Usually, that was all it took. The right mindset and a positive attitude.

A couple with a stroller stopped to look at the tiny faux fur vests Allie had hung above the counter.

She smiled, then let them take their time perusing the displays while their baby slept at their side.

"Five are already dead and a bunch more were injured," the man said, staring at his phone and speaking to the woman. "Two bombs in three days. Both at public locations. Businesses. Like this one," he said, raising his hands to motion around them. "It doesn't make any sense to be here today. Especially not with Chloe. She shouldn't have to be in harm's way because you got a little time off work."

The woman rolled her eyes and continued flipping through hangers. "No one is bombing the mall. Pull it together already. If someone was going to bomb the mall, they would have closed it."

"If it worked like that, they would've closed the real-estate office and Burger Mania." He pushed the stroller behind her, clearly distressed as she rounded the kiosk's corner.

Allie worked up a warm smile when the couple looked her way. Max had said the same thing last night. He'd wanted her to stay home today, but how could she? The bills wouldn't pay themselves. And bomber or no bomber, Allie wanted to see Baby Threads succeed. She wanted to make it on her own. Without needing Max's help to get by.

The man laughed at something the woman said, then dropped a kiss on her forehead. "Humor me," he said. "Let's do what you came here to do and leave. We can spend the rest of the day at home. You can rest. I'll make lunch and watch after Chloe."

The woman froze. Her gaze flicked to Allie, then back to the man. "Deal." She stacked the items from her hand onto the counter in front of Allie. "We'll take these. I have the sudden urge to go home." She pulled the man's mouth to hers and pressed a kiss against it while Allie tallied up the total.

She smiled at the couple as they walked away, ignoring the pinch of regret in her gut. She and Max had had days like that once, and she missed those times terribly.

Truthfully, she missed *him* terribly. Even when

he called at three in the morning demanding she leave town. It was kind of nice to know he still worried about her.

Allie yawned. Desperately in need of sleep.

Her ex-husband was clearly still in her head, because she swore she saw him approaching through the crowd. She strained for a clearer look at the fierce expression on an absurdly handsome face. Could it be? The resemblance was uncanny, right down to that towering presence that had always made him feel so much larger than life.

She narrowed her eyes as she took him in. Specifically the distinct gait in his walk, the result of a pretty high-tech artificial limb. She'd know that walk anywhere. He used to call the prosthesis his bionic leg to make her laugh. He wasn't wrong. The piece came complete with a battery-powered ankle that functioned a lot like a real one. Her favorite part about it had always been the man who got up every day, put it on and got to work. Because nothing stopped Max from protecting people. Not even losing part of himself, and nearly his life, to the cause.

Butterflies flew wildly in her stomach at the realization, and heat flushed instantly over every part of her. It was completely unfair that even now, after eight months of divorce, he had the same impact on her as the day they'd first met.

She tugged the ends of her too-curly hair and wished she'd taken more time with it this morning. *Dumb*, she complained internally. Why did she have to spend precious time on her unruly locks to feel attractive when Max woke up looking like that?

He smiled as he crossed the final few feet to her kiosk, the same devilish and dangerous smile that had pulled her in three years ago. One she'd yet to develop an immunity to, it seemed. "Allie."

"Max." She squared her shoulders and smiled politely back, willing her traitorous body not to go in for a hug.

"You look good," he said, taking a moment to drag his gaze over her.

"Thank you." She bit her tongue against the urge to tell him he looked good, too. This wasn't a casual visit between friends. This was an ambush. He'd asked her by phone not to come to work, and she'd ignored him. So he had come in person to press his point.

She crossed her arms and waited, trying not to get hung up on the way his rich brown skin and tawny eyes had always seemed straight off a billboard, or the way the added stubble on his cheeks begged for her touch.

"About our talk last night," he said, casting a careful look at the shoppers around her kiosk.

"I guess Director Suzuki agreed with your request." Allie wasn't surprised. He'd told her about his plan to contact the TCD director and ask to get the team involved in the local bombing case. He'd wanted to come to Grand Rapids. And Max always got his way.

Except when he'd told her to stay home today, so here he was, working on that.

"Doing a little after-Christmas shopping before you get to work?" she asked.

He frowned, and her gut twisted as another possibility rushed into mind. Could he be there because he was right? Was there a bomb in the mall? Her gaze swept over the masses around them. Friends and families. Young and old. Her stomach dropped and the chill of fear raised gooseflesh on her arms.

"I just wanted to see you," he said, stopping her erratic train of thought before it completely derailed. He leaned an elbow on the narrow counter beside her and flashed an irresistible grin. "Remind you that I have a pretty great condo in Traverse City that you and Max Jr. would really enjoy."

The shoppers moved around him, comparing items and prices from her kiosk while obviously eavesdropping.

Allie smiled sweetly back. "That's very nice of you, but like I said before, I can't. I have to work. These Baby Threads don't make themselves." She cast a congenial look at the shoppers.

When she turned her attention back to Max, her heart gave a heavy thud. There was pain in his fathomless brown eyes and frustration in the set of his jaw. "You should reconsider," he said, moving into her personal space. "You deserve a few days away. I'm sure that's all it will take."

"No."

Max pressed his lips tight, and she imagined kissing them open. He smelled like heat and spice and man.

She gave herself a few hearty internal kicks. "But I'm glad you're here. I was hoping to talk to you about something."

The remaining kiosk shoppers headed for the escalator, leaving her alone with her greatest, most infuriating temptation.

Max watched them go, then flicked his eyes back to her. "I know you think I'm trying to tell you what to do," he said softly, leaning in close to keep their conversation private. "I'm trying to protect you."

Allie shivered at the intensity of his voice, overcome with memories of other emotion-packed moments shared between them. Of promises made and vows exchanged. Her heart ached at once for all they'd lost. Her. Max. And their son.

"Both targets have been public locations," Max continued, dragging her mind back to reality. "Just like the mall. I'd feel better if you were home with Max. More so if you both left the city until I find this guy and haul him in."

She sighed. "I'm staying right here, and Max and I aren't leaving town. But I thought of something this morning I wanted to run by you. It's probably nothing, but I know you think everything is something, and you're usually right."

He smiled.

She shook her head, feeling a senseless heat rise in her cheeks. How she'd missed that smile.

Allie relayed her story about the late-night trip

to the drugstore and apologized for her inability to talk or think straight when he'd called. Then she got to the detail that had been haunting her all morning.

"I was stopped at the light on Burns and Hughes when the bomb went off at Burger Mania. I had a clear view of the building, but I was too far away to make out anything specific or useful. The blast woke Max Jr." She sighed, exhaustion tugging at her once more. "It was scary and more than a little surreal. I just sat there when the light changed. I was the only car on the street, and it took a minute to pull my addled thoughts together. At first, I couldn't make sense of what I was seeing. Then I remembered the news story about the realty office, and I realized someone had set off a bomb. I tried to quiet Max Jr. I shushed and sang. I pulled ahead when I noticed the light was green. Then I saw this man on the sidewalk. He just stared at me as I drove past. There was something in his expression. I thought it was shock. Maybe he was a witness, like me." She bit her lip, wondering if her constant internal desire to be useful was planting ideas where there were no grounds.

Max shifted, crossing his arms and rubbing his chin with long, steady fingers. "You think he could've been the bomber."

She pressed her lips together and shrugged. "Maybe."

"You got a good look at him?"

Allie nodded. She'd seen the man's face constantly in her mind since she woke this morning.

"You can describe him?"

Another nod. "Even if he was just a witness, he was closer to the building than I was when the blast happened. He was outside instead of in a car, and he wasn't distracted by a miserable little boy. He could have vital information either way."

Max worked his jaw, clenching and releasing the muscles. "I'll tell the team and local PD. You should meet with a sketch artist as soon as possible. Until then, what can you tell me about him? I can pass that on, as well."

Allie brought the stranger's image easily back to mind. "He was about five foot ten. Late thirties. Unkempt hair, too long for the cut. He had a beard, maybe two weeks' worth. And he wore one of those shapeless, hip-length coats." She touched her hips as a visual. "It was black with big rectangular pockets on each side of the zipper in front. And I could see the wool or fleece lining around the collar and inside the hood. Pale gray or dirty white. I don't know."

"That's good. All of that helps. A sketch artist will bring it to life, but this will get us started," Max said. "I'm going to head over to the station. I'll pass this information on when I meet with the team. Think about that condo in Traverse City."

She crossed her arms over her chest, fighting the sensation of infinite loss. "Go on," she said as warmly as possible and forcing a smile. "Get out of here and catch this guy. Then neither of us will have to worry anymore."

Without thinking, she rose onto her toes and pressed a kiss to his stubble-covered cheek. Her hand rested briefly on his sculpted chest, and his heart beat steadily against her palm.

Max's hand covered hers as she rocked back onto her heels, capturing her fingers against his shirt. The intensity in his gaze was enough to double her heart rate and buckle her knees. The heat in his touch, the contrast of his large hand holding her smaller one. She shivered.

"Can I come over tonight?" he asked, his voice deep and low.

Allie's jaw sank open. She wanted to say, *Yes!* And *No!* And *Yippee!* But only a little squeak sound came out.

"I'd like to see Max Jr.," he clarified. "If that's okay with you."

Her hearty exhalation turned to soft laughter. "Of course." He wanted to see their son. Like a good father would. And Max was an excellent father, even with the distance she'd put between them when she'd moved closer to her parents.

She wiggled her hand free from his grip, then stuffed her tingling fingers into her pocket. "You're welcome anytime, Max."

He nodded, a fresh smile blooming on his ridiculously attractive face. "All right. I guess I'll see you tonight."

And she hoped, naively, that this time he might really show up.

Chapter Three

Max left the mall with hope and a headache. Hope, because Allie's unexpected information might lead to a quick arrest and save the city from further bombings. A headache, because he still wanted her to take Max Jr. and leave town until the bomber was under arrest. Max had known better than to think he could change Allie's mind on the spot, but he'd had to try. That was one of their fundamental differences. He always erred on the side of caution, and she always assumed he was overreacting. Which he wasn't.

Allie thought she was the levelheaded one. She never rushed to take shelter from storms or hurried to merge with traffic when her lane ended in a mile. Why? She still had a mile. She wasn't hasty or rash, and she loved telling him to relax. She always thought there was more time. Ironically, Max had thought there was still time to save their marriage, and he'd been wrong.

He checked the clock on his dashboard as he made his way across town to the Grand Rapids Police Department. He should've stayed at the mall a little longer, pushed harder for her to take his advice. He should have insisted. Or begged. Whatever it took, because now he was running late and heavily distracted.

It hadn't helped that she'd looked so damn good. Her fuzzy sweater clung in all the right places and so had her nicely fitting jeans. She'd looked soft and smelled like all his best memories. The deep green of her top had made her hazel eyes glow, and he'd imagined running his fingers through the soft blond curls tumbling over her shoulders. The fantasies had gotten more specific the closer he got to her, making it impossible to argue properly. He'd been lost in her stare, wanting to say everything he'd never been able to say before and wondering what she thought of him now. Did she still see him as the broken and emotionally unavailable fool who'd let her and Max Jr. down?

And what had caused the fantastic blush that had spread across her cheeks before he left? He'd asked to stop by and see Max Jr., but she'd clearly been thinking of something else. Did it have anything to do with him?

He could count that as one more thing guaranteed to circle his brain until he saw her again. Allie might've divorced him eight months ago, but she'd surely still be the death of him. He was lucky he hadn't crashed his SUV just thinking about her in that damn sweater.

Max hit his turn signal with a groan, then slid into an open space at the GRPD lot.

The Grand Rapids Police Department was located in a squat but sprawling one-story facility on the edge of town. It was nondescript, without bells or whistles. Just a big sign and a whole lot of traditional black-and-white cruisers out front. He entered through the main doors and introduced himself at the desk inside. The female officer gave him an appreciative once-over as she pointed him in the right direction.

"Thank you." He made his way through the mix of uniformed officers and others in suits or plain clothes. The familiar white noise was a comfort, and he felt his muscles begin to unwind. Another reason Allie had left him. Sometimes work felt more like home than his home. How could anyone blame him? He'd been serving nearly half the years he'd been alive. First with the military, then with the TCD. Somewhere along the line he'd forgotten how to be present in an off-the-clock moment, and it had cost him.

He spotted Axel and Carly outside an open doorway and knew he'd found the right place. He'd passed all his team members' vehicles on his way in and could only hope they weren't waiting for him to begin.

"Hey," Axel said, lifting a logoed disposable cup in greeting. "You made it."

Max nodded at his buddy, then at Carly, the

team's biological warfare specialist with her person-
alized travel mug. "Hope I'm not holding things up."

"No," Carly assured him, a warm smile on her
face. "We're waiting for Rihanna and the local law-
enforcement representatives. I'm loitering out here
to avoid sitting again after that drive."

"Same," Axel said, watching Max with trained
eyes. "No luck with Allie, I guess?"

"Not in the way I'd hoped, but she had some interesting information I think we should look into a
little further." He relayed the details of the man on
the street outside Burger Mania just after the blast.

Axel jotted the information down, then excused
himself and headed for the closed door at the end
of the hallway, marked Chief Drees.

Max slipped into the conference room, ready to
get the investigation started. It was time to get his
head in the game. Find the bomber. Haul him in.
Then it wouldn't matter if Allie and Max Jr. wanted
to live full-time at the mall or any other public place.

He slowed his steps to examine the unfamiliar
space and seating options. The area was roughly
half the size and thirty times the age of the team's
sleek high-tech boardroom back in Traverse City.
The conference table and chairs were easily older
than Max, and in lieu of a giant SMART board,
an old-fashioned projector screen had been pulled
down from a roll overhead and secured to a marker
tray by a string.

Max took the open seat across from Aria and
Selena, both of whom were engrossed with their

phones, likely reviewing the materials Opaline had provided earlier. Max had already committed the pertinent details to memory. There wasn't much so far, and he was waiting for her to work her magic and send more information soon.

Axel and Carly entered a moment later with the TCD liaison, Rihanna Clark, and a trio of local lawmen on their heels.

"Good morning. Again," Rihanna said with a grin. "I'm glad to see everyone made it safely. I'm going to jump right in with introductions so you can get to work." She outstretched a palm toward the men who'd filed in beside her. "These are the faces you'll want to look for if you need anything while you're here. Grand Rapids police chief Martin Drees, Detective Isaac Fohl and Sergeant Jim Sims, bomb squad."

Each man nodded and forced a smile at the sound of his name.

Rihanna then turned to the table. "And here we have the FBI's Traverse City Tactical Crime Division. Our supervisory agent is Axel Morrow." She lifted a palm in Axel's direction. "Going around the table from there we have Special Agent Aria Calletti, Special Agent Dr. Carly Welsh, Special Agent Selena Lopez and Special Agent Max McRay. Max is our explosives expert, and he'll be taking point on this case."

"Thank you," the police chief said, spending a moment to look each of the TCD members in the eyes. His white hair and face full of wrinkles suggested he was somewhere near Max's dad's age. The tightness around his eyes and mouth spoke of stress, fatigue and determination. He was a man who cared about people, his city and his job. "We appreciate you coming here and getting involved like this. We've never faced a serial bomber, and our citizens are on edge. The phones haven't stopped ringing since we announced the second explosion this morning. A number of school districts have reported record low attendance. Parents don't want to send their kids in case this nut goes for one of our schools next. I need to give the people of Grand Rapids some assurance of safety. And soon, or we'll have widespread panic on our hands."

Axel leaned forward, hands clasped on the table before him. "We understand, Chief Drees, and we'll do all we can to wrap this up quickly. Our goal is to bring the bomber in without any further incidents. Do you have any new leads or information available?"

"No." The chief shook his head, visibly deflated. "Aside from what you told me a few moments ago, none."

Axel turned to the team and shared the details Allie had given Max.

Chief Drees nodded along. "I've put in a call to our best sketch artist. I hope to have the image in all of your hands by this time tomorrow, if not before."

"That's good," Axel said. "Until then, we've got our best tech working hard on this case, as well, and I'm certain she'll have more for us to go on soon." His smile spread to the other team members at the mention of Opaline. He was right to praise her. Opaline was the queen of finding needles in haystacks, and when she was looking for someone, they couldn't hide.

The chief gave an appreciative nod, then turned to the doorway, where a uniformed officer had arrived with a clipboard and expectant expression.

The chief lifted a hand to the room, nodded, then took his leave, exiting the room with the waiting officer.

Detective Fohl pulled out a chair and had a seat at the table.

Sergeant Sims, the local bomb-squad leader, folded his arms but remained standing, his expression grim. "Good morning." Sergeant Sims was young and visibly exhausted. From the looks of him, Max would guess he probably hadn't slept more than a few hours since the first bomb blast.

The team returned the greeting in near unison.

Sims pushed a handful of shaggy brown hair off his forehead, and it sprang immediately back. His clothes were rumpled and his posture slack. "There's nothing new to report on the bomb front. We haven't been able to identify anything significant about the devices. Standard pressure-cooker style. Nothing unique or telling. No special signature to set the bomber's works apart. Nothing to trace back to the maker." He rubbed his eyes hard with one hand, then turned to his counterpart. "Detective Fohl has a little more for you."

The detective opened a manila folder and passed a stack of papers around. "This is a compilation of all the victims' names so far. Casualties first, then the injured. They're sorted further by the blast location." He removed a second stack of papers and circulated them around, as well. "These are the lists of all current employees for both businesses, as well as the names of people who were fired from either in the last six months."

Axel took one of each paper, then handed them along. "We'll want to push that back to a year for good measure." He raised his eyes to Rihanna, who nodded.

"I'll reach out to the businesses," she said, tapping her thumbs against her phone screen. "I'll get an updated list to you within the hour."

"Thanks," Axel said, before returning his attention to the detective. "Is there anyone with a grudge against one or more of the victims?"

The older man narrowed his eyes. "Nothing for certain, but I've spoken to both businesses about the employees who've left or been let go." He inclined his head to indicate the papers in Axel's grip. "There's been a greater amount of turnover at Burger Mania than at the real-estate office, as you can imagine. So we started looking into employees who left the real-estate office first. There were only three. Two were fired. One of those is currently in the hospital, recovering from a surgery. The other moved south and began a new career in landscaping. The last guy left of his own volition, but he did it with a stink, made a big scene. And as far as we can tell, he doesn't appear to have taken another job since."

Aria cocked her head. "Two solid alibis and one wild card," she said, voicing Max's thoughts.

Selena sighed dramatically, her smile widening. "We love a wild card." She slid her fingertip over the page before her, presumably down the short list of former employee names. "Which one is unaccounted for?"

The detective shifted forward, gaze intense. "Fritz O'Lear, and we haven't been able to reach him by phone for comment."

"What do we know about him so far?" Max asked, his mind already running over the most well-known American bombers. *Kaczynski, McVeigh, Helder, Rudolph, Metesky.* All average. All white males. Varied ages.

"Not much," the detective admitted. "Caucasian. Male. Midthirties. Unmarried. No kids. No previous record. And apparently, currently unemployed."

Max stood, drawing the group's attention. He was ready to get out there and get started, and he knew exactly where to go. "Got an address on Mr. O'Lear?"

Chapter Four

Max climbed into the passenger side of Axel's official, TCD-issued SUV, the heat of fresh purpose burning away January's bitter cold. The sooner this bomber was stopped, the sooner Max's family and this town would be safe, and he had a gut feeling about this lead.

He hadn't been surprised to see Axel on his feet in the conference room a bare heartbeat after himself. He and Axel had always been connected that way, always on the same wavelength, and more often than not, they shared the same instinctive responses.

Axel typed O'Lear's address into the dashboard GPS, then pumped up the heat and adjusted the vents. "First thoughts on this guy?" he asked, shifting smoothly into Reverse and heading away from the police department.

Max released a heavy breath and a plume of white fog blew into the air before him. He rubbed a palm against his thigh. "A recently disgruntled guy, who left his job in a huff and hasn't found new work after months of unemployment? I don't like it. And

I really don't like that he's been unreachable so far. Could be irrelevant, but—"

"It doesn't feel that way," Axel said, completing his thought.

"Yeah." Max nodded. "As for the fast-food joint being across town and presumably unrelated to the real-estate office, we won't know until we ask some more questions. Could be that this guy is the link between the two. Any number of things could've taken him to that place, or maybe he's never been there and that bombing was a decoy to throw us off. That wouldn't mean he didn't have a problem with one of the employees who were targeted, or even a regular customer."

Axel took the next right, increasing his speed as local limits permitted and likely working out a dozen possible bomber-motivation scenarios in his mind.

Max's attention, however, was divided. "Allie shot me down this morning," he complained. "Straight off. As if I was ridiculous to even suggest a bomber in her city could impact her. Apparently, it's a big city, and she doesn't know the guy, so she's fine. Max Jr. is also fine." He gritted his teeth against a building rant. *The bomber hasn't been identified.* That was the problem. He could work in the kiosk beside hers, for all she knew.

Max rubbed his forehead and bit his tongue. Axel didn't need to sit through another rail-against-Allie. Though he would, Max knew, without question or complaint. Axel had listened to many similar tirades during and immediately after the divorce. Not before, because Max had never seen it coming. He was too engrossed in his work to acknowledge his home life was falling apart. And the consequence of that was divorce. He cringed internally at the awful little word. Max had thought divorce was some magical, powerful, permanent change to everything. The end of all things as he knew them. He was wrong.

Max's divorce from Allie had only changed a few things, and all for the worse. She and Max Jr. were no longer at home when he got there. He'd lost the companionship of his best friend, his lover and life partner. He'd lost the only woman he'd ever imagined in any of those roles and the sixteen-month-old son whose every breath he cherished. Now Max was on his own, and loathing the bachelorhood he'd once stupidly worried he might miss after marriage. But despite the things divorce had changed, everything else was exactly the same. The sun still rose and set. Max still filled the bulk of his waking hours with work, and he still loved Allie as fiercely as ever. He felt protective of her, thrilled by the sight of her and frustrated as hell by her earlier dismissal. Max wasn't a jealous man, wasn't overbearing or unreasonable. And bombs were his life's work. So when he suggested she take Max Jr. and get out of town for a few days, he'd hoped she would listen.

"Well, maybe we'll get lucky," Axel said. "O'Lear will be our man. He'll confess everything at the sight of us. We'll haul him in, and Allie, Max Jr. and the rest of this city will be safe before lunch."

Max snorted. "If only." He stared through his window at the fittingly bleak, gray day. "I'm not usually that lucky." A phantom limb pain pinched and ached in his missing calf, as if on cue. He'd learned years ago not to reach for it, not to try to soothe it. The pain wasn't real. The limb wasn't there. And he wasn't sure if his subconscious was agreeing or disagreeing with his lack of luck by reminding him of the bombing that had nearly ended his life. He'd lost part of his leg in the blast, but he'd lived, and that made him luckier than too many others.

Max's thoughts cleared, and his vision pulled tight on his reflection in the glass. Not only had he survived, but he'd gone on to meet and fall in love with Allie. They'd married and had a son he adored. Had Max died, he wouldn't be in Grand Rapids now, willing to do whatever it took to protect his family and to keep this bomber from taking a single additional life.

The bomber, he realized, was the unlucky one.

Axel slid the SUV against the curb in a low-income neighborhood a few minutes later. "Not the most impressive residence for a recent Realtor," he said, drawing Max back to the moment.

They stared at the bland yellow-brick building, across a sea of filthy snow and a poorly shoveled walkway. Everything about the property was in need of repair.

Max expanded his scan of the area, moving from the stout three-story building, to neighboring homes and apartments, the street, parked and moving vehicles as well as the sporadic and partially frozen pedestrians hurrying in every direction. "I thought Realtors made a good living."

"Only if they make enough commissions. O'Lear must not have sold enough homes to afford a better place or keep his job. Which suggests he's not a people person. You have to possess a certain set of skills to part people from their money. The fact that the agency let him go is a red flag. Most Realtors are like freelancers, not salaried, and as long as they bring in money for the agency, I'd think staff would overlook some rough-around-the-edges behavior."

Max stepped onto the sidewalk and bundled his coat tighter as Axel joined him. They strode quickly, purposefully, to the tenement. Axel rang the buzzer for O'Lear's apartment. When no one answered, he pressed the button again. Then repeatedly, until a young woman in running shoes and earbuds, her hood up and eyes down, emerged from the locked door and began a jog down the broken sidewalk.

Max's arm snapped out, catching the door before it closed behind her.

"See? Luck," Axel said, stepping into the building's narrow first-floor foyer.

The space was cluttered. A bank of mailboxes lined one wall and a scattering of abandoned fast-food bags, a deflated playground ball and a pair of children's sneakers littered the floor. It wasn't much warmer inside than outside.

Max and Axel climbed the stairs to the third floor,

breathing stale, sour air. The scents of garbage, grease and something like marijuana burned through Max's nose and down his throat. He could only imagine the stench during warmer months.

Axel reached O'Lear's door first and knocked. Chin up and shoulders back, the thirty-four-year-old looked like someone not to be trifled with, and it suited him. At six foot two, Axel was taller than the average criminal, fit to a fault and trained in hand-to-hand combat. His wool dress coat, shiny shoes and easy smile left some room for confusion in dumber bad guys. Their tendencies to underestimate him always resulted in Axel's upper hand.

Max could count the number of dress pants and shiny shoes in his closet on one hand, and he rarely wore either to work, never into the field. He was just as tall as Axel, broader and rarely underestimated. He scanned the hall as Axel knocked again, more loudly this time.

Torn and stained carpeting ran underfoot, frayed along broken baseboards and cut off at doorjambs by dented metallic strips. Televisions blared from nearby apartments, accented by warbling voices, a muffled baby's cry and a barking dog.

Only silence filtered through O'Lear's door.

Max tried again, knocking louder and announcing "Delivery! Package for Mr. O'Lear." Still nothing.

Axel stepped back, lips drawn briefly to one side. "Nobody's home. Try again in a few hours?"

"Yep." Max turned back to the stairs with a sigh. He knew their luck had a limit.

The ride to the station passed quickly. There was less traffic and no underlying anticipation. No possibility that they were about to face off with a serial bomber on his turf.

The station was busy, and the cops stared, curiosity plain in their collective gaze. Any officers who hadn't been on duty when the TCD arrived were probably just hearing about the team from Traverse City who'd commandeered their conference room until further notice. Max was sure it must be strange for hosting officers. He nodded and greeted as many as possible. Since they were seen as interlopers, stealing a case the locals could've handled themselves wouldn't bode well when the TCD needed assistance navigating local customs, laws or culture.

A familiar woman's voice spilled through the open conference-room doorway as Rihanna appeared. She smiled at the sight of Max and Axel. "You're just in time. Opaline's on a conference call, and I was about to close the door."

The men ducked inside, neither willing to miss a single word of Opaline's report.

Her warm smile centered a large screen, thanks to a laptop connected to the precinct's projector.

Max smiled, despite himself, in return.

Opaline's head and shoulders were larger than life, the tips of her bleached-blond bangs flamed blue. A perfect match for her eye makeup and glittery top. Hot-pink lips glowed against her light skin.

The woman knew how to turn heads, and words like *low-key* and *nondescript* were lost in her presence.

Max had always appreciated Opaline's silver-lining attitude, especially on days he could only see the storm. Divorced, like Max, Opaline knew what it meant to lose someone to the demands of the TCD. Unlike him, however, Opaline dated. Frequently and with great hope. Max didn't see the point. Not when he knew there was only one woman for him, and he'd already wrecked things with her.

The buzzing room quieted as Max and Axel took their seats. Rihanna dimmed the lights, and Opaline became impossibly brighter in the drab, somewhat cramped confines of the Grand Rapids PD conference room.

The entire team was present. Good news for time and efficiency. Everyone would be able to respond and weigh in, then build off one another's opinions, views and suggestions. Launching the investigation in the best possible way. Max nodded to himself. Maybe his luck wasn't all bad. If O'Lear had been home, Max and Axel would've been tied up with him and possibly missed something paramount.

"Hello." Opaline waved on the screen. "I just wanted to touch base and see if you have anything new for me since this morning, and also to let you know what I've got going over here on my end. I'm currently running background checks on all employees for both businesses from the past year. I'm looking into employee records, school records, past jobs, local family and friends, favorite restaurants, hobbies, gyms or anything else I can use to make a connection between the two businesses. I don't have anything yet, but something will turn up, if I have to trace every one of their lives back to preschool."

Max's knee bobbed, unbidden, as adrenaline pooled, desperate for an outlet. Opaline didn't have anything yet. His gaze darted around the room as she continued her update. He found some solace in the fact every team member wore the same expression, looking a lot like he felt. Frustrated. Anxious. Eager and determined to stop the bomber.

"So you reached out to let us know you don't know anything?" Selena, Opaline's sister, asked, her tone unnecessarily harsh and thick with sarcasm.

"I'm working on it," Opaline said, her smile bright but tight. "I always check in frequently in situations like these because everything can change in an instant. You know that."

Max had no idea what the beef was between the Lopez siblings, but today wasn't the day to sort it out. "Do you have lists of the victims' local family and friends?" Max asked.

Opaline took a beat to compose herself and return to the task at hand. Her fingers flew across her keyboard in the silence. "Absolutely. I'm emailing those to you now."

Phones buzzed and vibrated across the conference room.

Max swiped his cell phone to life, quickly accessing the new information. "Let's split up and interview as many of these people as possible. We'll regroup afterward and see if any names come up on both sides of this. We're looking for someone with a connection to one or more of the victims in each blast."

His teammates raised their phones, too, accessing the lists and talking rapidly among themselves.

"Opaline," Max continued. "I think the times of the blast were significant, as well. The bomber didn't choose one time for both attacks, so I'm guessing the times had more to do with the locations or intended victims than the bomber's schedule. Why two a.m. at the burger joint and seven eighteen a.m. at the real-estate office? Can we find out who was typically present at those specific times and possibly work from there to find a common denominator?"

Carly tapped her pink nails against the table, thin brows furrowed. "Vengeance killings."

Max dipped his chin in agreement, as did the other agents seated at the table. "I think so. Someone with an ax to grind and multiple possible offenders."

Tension pulled Carly's expression tight. "Unlimited offenders," she corrected him. "A guy this unstable likely has a lot of perceived enemies, real or imagined, and unless he had a problem with all the people he hurt at Burger Mania, we can assume he doesn't care if bystanders are hurt, or worse, in the process. If he goes after someone working at a large or busy venue, the collateral damage could be hundreds. We have to hope his next target isn't employed by a concert hall or sports arena."

Or a mall, Max thought, his stomach dropping to the floor.

Rihanna cleared her throat and peeled herself away from the door, where she'd taken up residence. As the team liaison, she often stayed on her feet during meetings. Continually on alert and prepared to deal with local law enforcement, press or the public as needed. Her diligence made it possible for the team to work with limited interruptions. "I thought you might say that." She grinned at Carly as she slid a stack of papers onto the conference table. "I've set up meetings with real-estate office employees and the victims' families."

Opaline beamed. "Excellent. You guys work on that. I'll keep pushing my way through this. And we'll chat again soon." She reached for the screen, then vanished.

The team passed Rihanna's pages around, pairing up and hovering over the text.

Selena muttered something under her breath, presumably about her sister, as she scanned the paper. Beside her, Aria locked her attention on Max. "Selena and I can talk with the real-estate office employees, if you want."

Max nodded, pulling his gaze back to Axel. "Why don't we visit the victims' family members?"

Axel stood as Selena and Aria pushed away from the table. "Call between interviews," he instructed. "Even if it's just to say the conversation was a bust.

As you know, communication is paramount in these early hours."

Max pulled up the rear as the group headed for the parking lot, eager to start making progress on the case.

Chapter Five

Aria slid behind the wheel of her SUV and waited as Selena got comfortable in the passenger seat. Ramsey Realty was across town from the police station, and in a situation like this one, time wasn't on the TCD's side. Every moment the bomber went unchecked was another minute he had to plan—or worse, to execute—his next attack.

Aria motored along the snow-lined streets, following GPS directions and hoping to make significant progress with the interviews.

Selena looked over her shoulder every few minutes, into the empty back seat, then frowned again.

"Missing Blanca?" Aria asked.

Blanca, the white German shepherd and K-9 officer, was Selena's partner, and the bond between the two was immeasurable. Being away from her for this case had left Selena visibly on edge, like a mother away from a newborn. Though Blanca was about as helpless as a baby honey badger. Aria knew the feeling, already missing her fiancé, Grayson, and their precious infant, Danny.

"It's weird without her," Selena admitted, facing forward once more. "I keep forgetting she's not there, and it feels like I'm missing an appendage."

Blanca was back in Traverse City, cashing in on some well-deserved time off. Much as Selena had hated to leave her, it hadn't made sense to bring Blanca on this case. She wasn't trained to locate bombs or identify accelerants, so she'd have spent all her time in the freezing cold vehicle, or in a pen at an unfamiliar station.

Aria parked in the Ramsey Realty lot, outside the partially ruined single-story brick building. Yellow crime-scene tape circled the structure, and several signs warned the public to stay back. A corporate trailer had been set up a few yards from the building's front door. A vinyl banner along the side proclaimed, Yes! We're Open! And a Ramsey Realty sign had been attached to the handrail of a small retractable set of steps. "I guess this is the place."

Aria and Selena made their way across the freshly plowed lot, then let themselves into the trailer. The stale air was tinged with cinnamon, and muffled voices carried through a paper-thin interior wall.

"Hello?" Aria called, moving toward the nearest empty desk. The nameplate said Susan Myer. Steam lifted from a mug near a stack of papers, and the computer was powered on. "Susan?"

Quick footfalls tapped along the tile floor in their direction. "Coming!" a bright voice returned. "Sorry," she said, rounding the corner toward her desk with a wide smile. "I didn't hear you come in. The coffee maker is a little persnickety back there, and I did my best to help, though only time will tell."

She paused to assess the agents, and her smile fell. Susan had likely seen enough law officials in the past few days to know a pair when they appeared before her. She pulled in a deep breath. "How can I help you?"

"We're Special Agents Calletti and Lopez," Aria explained. "We'd like to ask you some questions about the bombing."

Susan fell gracelessly into the seat at her desk. "Of course." She lifted her mug with slightly trembling hands. She was too polished for the trailer. From her one-piece black jumpsuit and heels, to her high-end haircut and professionally manicured nails, everything about her clashed with the underwhelming surroundings. "What would you like to know?"

Selena motioned toward the rumble of voices. "Who else is here?"

"Bailey and Frank," Susan answered. "They're hoping for coffee."

Selena nodded, then headed silently in the direction from which Susan had come.

"I'm sorry for your loss," Aria said, her attention focused on the woman at her desk. "I know what it feels like to lose coworkers. We see our teammates more hours a day than our families." Her heart ached at the thought. For Aria, this sort of loss was inevitable, if she stayed on the job long enough. Death was one of those things all first responders accepted long before taking the oath or earning the badge.

But not Realtors. Not Susan or the Burger Mania workers. These folks had signed on to sell homes and provide cheap, fast food. They'd never imagined this day could come. And Aria couldn't imagine that kind of blow.

Selena returned with a middle-aged man wearing a logoed polo shirt and khaki pants, and a woman in a gray sweater dress. "Frank Thomas, Bailey White, this is Special Agent Calletti."

Aria nodded in greeting. "Nice to meet you both. Agent Lopez has probably already told you we're here to follow up on the bombing at your office. Would you like to sit while we talk?"

The Realtors moved silently to a pair of desks beyond Susan's, catching their coworker's eyes as they passed.

Frank's fingers curled at his sides. "Tell me you have a lead on the maniac who did this."

"We're working on it." Aria scanned each face carefully, waiting for signs someone knew more than they'd want to announce in a group. The sting of cinnamon air freshener intensified as the trailer's heater kicked on, blowing loudly over them. "Our team is here to pursue the matter full-time until the culprit is apprehended."

Selena moved to Aria's side. "Any idea who'd do something like this?"

The trio of employees shook their heads.

Selena waited before speaking again. A practice Aria used often. When no one blurted anything under the pressure of silence, she continued. "Anyone have a problem with your company, the office manager or Realtor who was caught in the blast?"

Susan frowned. "Maybe Fritz. He didn't come to mind right away, because he hasn't been here in months, but he wasn't happy when he left." She cast her gaze to her fellow real-estate workers.

"Maybe," Frank mumbled. "I don't know. Was he smart enough to do something like this? Isn't building bombs hard?"

Selena's gaze flicked briefly to Aria.

Aria's instincts went on alert. Fritz wasn't a common name, and it had come up earlier in the team meeting. Not a coincidence.

Selena lifted her chin. "Tell me about Fritz."

Susan straightened her posture, apparently accepting the role of spokesperson. "Fritz O'Lear was an agent here, briefly. We hired him in a pinch and regretted it almost immediately. He interviewed well, if a little flat on personality. But it takes all kinds to sell homes. Some of the fussier buyers don't like Realtors with too much show and pizzazz—they complain we're just trying to sell them something."

Selena's eyebrows quirked slightly. "Aren't you? You're trying to sell houses."

"Sure, but that's not all we do." Susan bristled. "We're matchmakers on the front end, trying to find exactly what each customer wants for a price they can afford. On the back end we're investigators. Number crunchers. And liaisons. We work with area businesses and homeowners to prep and stage their homes for a quick sale while estimating fair market values and jumping through hoops for buyers. Fritz was good at the research and numbers."

"But?" Selena prompted when Susan didn't go on.

Frank leaned across his desk, hands folded. "No one liked him. People didn't want to work with him, and instead of asking for one of us to handle their search or sell, they'd just go with another realty firm. He was terrible for business."

Aria moved in Frank's direction, seeing the weak link among the three. "You didn't like him."

Frank shrugged. His chin jutted. "No. Not particularly. If he disagreed with you, he'd get insulting. And he couldn't take a joke, would always respond in a nasty way. Had a real chip on his shoulder. Would carry a grudge. It was clear he was that way around our clients, too, from feedback we got. So we told him maybe he'd be more comfortable at another firm, maybe a bigger one. You know, where he could do a lot of office and online stuff and not interact with the public as much."

"You think Fritz is capable of blowing up buildings?" she asked. "Assuming he could figure it out?" She narrowed her eyes, throwing back his earlier accusation that bomb-building was hard, and perhaps Fritz was stupid. "Is he capable of murder?"

"Maybe," Frank said, doing his best to seem indifferent when his posture and the flush of his skin betrayed him. "He was cussing everyone when he left. Throwing blame around like it was someone else's fault he couldn't sell homes."

"He was mad because you guys taunted him,"

Bailey said, suddenly finding her voice. Her cheeks pinkened and her gaze jerked to Aria. "Frank and Gary made fun of Fritz for his lack of sales. Even when Fritz had a good week, it was never enough. Never close to the number Gary sold, and they never let him forget it."

Frank gaped, then scowled. "You think this is my fault? I teased some guy a little, and his response is a killing spree?"

Bailey backed down, and Aria resisted the urge to dump Frank from his chair.

"Gary and our office manager were lost in the bombing," Susan said, gently rubbing her forehead.

Aria turned, thankful for a place to redirect her attention.

Selena's eyes flashed at the platinum blonde. "Gary was a Realtor who taunted Fritz, and I'm guessing the office manager is the one he faced off with when he turned in his notice?"

Susan nodded.

"Got a picture of Fritz?" Selena asked. "An old ad or mailer or something?"

Susan pursed her lips. "I'm afraid not. We handle our own promotions, and the company's print directory and materials were damaged in the explosion. But his photo was online with his listings. He's been gone a few months, but the internet is forever, right?"

Aria's thumbs were in action as Susan spoke, already digging up images of Fritz O'Lear outside homes with the Ramsey Realty sign. A clean-cut, fox-faced man in his thirties looked back at the camera, inauthentic smile in place. His light brown hair was laced with gray, and his small brown eyes were narrowly set against a long, broad nose. "This him?" she asked, turning the screen to face Susan, then sweeping it slowly in the direction of Bailey and Frank.

"Yes." The trio agreed.

Selena left her business card with Susan.

Aria gave one of her cards to Frank and one to Bailey. "Please keep this information to yourself. It's early in the case, and we don't want to tip off a potential bomber. Also, if you see Fritz O'Lear, do not approach. Call us. We're hoping to talk with him. Maybe rule him out."

Back in the cold, the agents moved quickly to the SUV. Selena's gaze swept to the rear window, where Blanca normally awaited her return.

Both of them knew of Max and Axel's assignment to locate O'Lear. That effort would have to intensify. But they had another location to visit.

"Burger Mania?" Aria asked, thankful for the lead and hoping for more good luck at stop number two.

"Burger Mania," Selena agreed.

Chapter Six

Max pulled Rihanna's notes from the glove box as Axel piloted the SUV into traffic. "We're two for two," he said, feeling more defeated than he liked this early in the game.

Of the families they'd visited so far, both had lost a loved one to the Burger Mania blast. Both families were wrecked, as expected, their conversations soaked in tears, anger and frustration. But no one had any idea who might've done such a thing. None of them seemed to remember a Fritz O'Lear or someone who looked like him.

"Where to next?" Axel asked, motoring toward the nearest main road.

"Sherman Oaks Parkway." Max tapped the address into the dashboard GPS, then settled back in his seat. "We're meeting with Jordyn Knightly's family. If they don't have anything to offer, we'll be out of leads."

Axel glanced at the GPS, then took the next turn. "What do we know about Jordyn?"

"Twenty-three, blond hair, brown eyes." Max

flipped the notes around in his hands, reading the limited details. "She worked the night shift at Burger Mania and attended classes at the community college during the day. Looks like she was born and raised in the area. Has immediate and extended family here in Grand Rapids. She shared an apartment with her best friend, Kia."

"Do we have Kia's address?" Axel asked.

"Yeah. It's with the details Opaline put together on Jordyn. We can try there next." At least that added one more thread of hope for the day. If Jordyn's family didn't have anything new to offer, maybe the young woman had confided something to her roommate that would help.

Axel slipped the SUV into Park several minutes later, beside a driveway with multiple cars.

The cottage-style home was covered in gray shake and lined in clean white trim.

Max unfastened his seat belt. "Well, we can eliminate the possibility that the attacks were based on socioeconomic reasons." The first victim's parents had both been physicians, and the second victim's family had lived in a housing project. This was a solid middle-class, blue-collar neighborhood.

"Agreed," Axel said.

Their phones buzzed with incoming texts. A message from Aria with a photograph of Fritz O'Lear in his Ramsey Realty jacket.

Max surveyed the photo. Allie hadn't recalled the hair or eye color of the man she'd seen outside Burger Mania, but it was hard to reconcile the description she'd given with the image before him. Maybe the unidentified man had been a witness after all.

"Looks like Aria and Selena are making more progress than we are," Axel said. "If we don't break this streak, we're going back empty-handed."

Max smiled. "Then we'd better get to work."

The agents met on the sidewalk and made their way up a snow-lined walkway to the small front porch. A cherry-red wreath hung on a cheery blue door.

"Maybe the third interview is the charm," Axel suggested, then began to knock.

A puffy-faced woman in rectangular glasses and a messy ponytail answered. "Yes?"

Max made the introductions, and the woman invited them inside.

A small collection of adults covered the couch and love seat beyond the door. They'd clearly overheard the exchange so far and had fallen silent in response.

"I'm Jocelyn," the puffy-faced woman said, closing the door behind them. "Jordyn was my beautiful little girl." A powerful sob racked her small frame as she spoke, then doubled her over at the couch's edge.

A man stood to collect her, guiding her to his vacated seat. "Sit, honey. Rest."

A younger woman with curly red hair rose from the love seat and pointed to the woman still seated there. "We're Sage and Grace. Jordyn's cousins. That's our mom, Alicia," she said, pointing to a woman who'd entered the room when Jocelyn had begun to cry, then froze at the sight of the agents. "On the couch is our dad, David, our brother Jim, and Kia, Jordyn's best friend. That's our uncle Brad, Jordyn's dad." She pointed to the man helping Jocelyn get settled.

Max nodded in greeting, thankful to see so many of Jordyn's loved ones in one place, especially Kia, the roommate. "We're very sorry for your loss." He let the words sit between them a moment, hoping to convey the fact he truly meant them. Max knew loss intimately. He'd lost more than his share to senseless acts of violence in the service. All were far too young, and each absence had left a mark on his heart. "We won't take up too much of your time. We just wanted to introduce ourselves and let you know our team is here now, working in conjunction with the local police department to identify and apprehend the person responsible for these bombings. We won't leave until we have justice for you and the others who've lost loved ones." He gave them another minute to process, then added, "We're very good at what we do."

Axel shifted, folding his hands in front of him. "Your local police haven't stopped following up, but it's easy for a force to spread themselves too thin in times like these. Our team, on the other hand, will devote one hundred percent of our time to this investigation, until we've seen it through. You have our complete attention."

Jocelyn wept loudly again, folding forward in

her seat on the couch. Her husband crouched before her, stroking her face and whispering words of encouragement.

"We're visiting everyone on the Burger Mania staff," Max said. "Looking for ideas about who could've done this. We'll follow every lead and suggestion to its end, and we never disclose how we came upon a name in conjunction to a crime. Is there anyone you can think of who might've had a problem with one of the victims? Maybe another employee or customer? An ex-spouse or significant other. Anything Jordyn might've told you that seemed extreme or worrisome?"

The group members looked at one another, eager and curious. Then their heads began to shake. No.

"Have you ever heard the name Fritz O'Lear?" Max asked. It was a long shot, but the only one they had at the moment, and worth tossing out there. Though the name hadn't registered to anyone at the last two homes he and Axel had visited.

Kia frowned, as if trying to recall, but didn't comment.

Jocelyn sat taller, her sobs quieted. "Is that the man who did this?" Her voice grew firm and angry. "Is he the monster who took my baby girl?"

Axel unfolded his hands and lifted his palms hip-high, then relaxed them at his sides as she calmed. "He worked at the realty office that was also bombed. We don't know if he's a victim, too. We're hoping to find links between the two targeted businesses. Did any of you have recent interactions with someone from Ramsey Realty? Did Jordyn?"

Max brought up the photo of O'Lear on his phone. "This is Fritz O'Lear." He passed the device to the women on the love seat and watched as they took turns looking, then passing it on.

When the phone reached Kia, her curious expression turned to confusion. "This is Fritz O'Lear?" She fished a phone from her purse and set Max's aside. A moment later, she turned her screen to him. "Could this be the same guy?"

Axel moved in closer as Kia handed Max both phones.

The agents compared a covertly captured image of a man leaving Burger Mania. His hair was longer than in the realty photo, and he had a bit of beard growth, but it was him, and in this more recent photo, Fritz was exactly as Allie had described. Right down to the black hip-length jacket with visible wool at the collar and large rectangular pockets on the chest.

"Jordyn sent me that," Kia said. "He came in a few times and was really nice at first. Typical for an older guy. Jordyn's beautiful, smart, kind. *Was*," she corrected herself, eyes filling with tears.

"Take your time," Max encouraged.

Jocelyn passed a box of tissues in Kia's direction.

The room was silent around them, all eyes on the girl with information everyone wanted.

Kia pressed a tissue to her nose and settled her breaths. "She took his order once, and they talked while the kitchen prepped whatever it was that he paid for. He kept coming back after that, but instead of sitting at the tables or stepping aside, he lingered, always wanting her time and attention. She started taking her breaks to avoid him, but he'd stick around, drinking coffee and waiting until she had to go back to the register. Then he'd approach her. Eventually, he asked her out. It was like he couldn't see she was ghosting him. She turned him down politely, but it didn't stop him. He kept coming in, hanging around, watching her. Then he asked her out again a couple weeks ago. She'd had it with all the nights of feeling uncomfortable because of him. She said it was like she was being punished for ever having that first conversation."

"She said no again?" Max guessed.

Kia nodded. "Yeah. He really creeped her out."

"Wait a minute," Jocelyn said. She scooted to the edge of the couch, tears dried and her husband's handkerchief clutched in her hands. "I remember this. A couple weeks ago, Jordyn told me about an older man who asked her out at work. I told her to report him for making her uncomfortable, and to tell him to shove off!" Jocelyn turned wide eyes on the agents. "He was pushy the second time. Didn't want to take no for an answer. He told her, 'C'mon, give me a chance.'" Jocelyn covered her mouth, tears spilling freely again. "She was firm, like I told her. She told him to pay attention. Her answer was no, and it wouldn't change. When he kept going, she asked if his brain was on the fritz. Like his name."

Her husband pulled her back, his expression crumbling now. Strength gone.

Max thanked them, told them they'd been helpful, but warned them that this Fritz guy might just be a witness and not involved. He didn't want any of them going for vigilante justice, after all.

Max passed his business card to Kia. Then he and Axel let themselves out.

They'd identified a prime suspect. Now they just had to find him.

Chapter Seven

Allie added a second swipe of mascara to her lashes and drove the lip-gloss wand around her red lips once more. She'd changed into her most flattering pair of jeans and chosen a fitted red turtleneck to accent the work she'd been doing at the gym. Max had caught her off guard at the mall, but not tonight. Tonight, she was determined to give him the same thrill he'd given her at the sight of him. Even after all these months apart, one look at Max sent her back to the moments of their early days together. Butterflies in the stomach. Heat in her chest and cheeks. And damn it all, he knew her secret. He was trained to see the subtle changes that broke like fireworks against her fair, freckled skin.

Her heart hammered at the memory of his nearness. His strong, authoritative voice. His broad, sexy chest. Muscular arms and hands that knew exactly what she liked. She'd imagined kissing his lips a thousand times since he'd walked away from her at the mall. Heard his sweet whispers against her ear. Felt the warmth of his embrace. As if he was still hers.

As if he'd ever *really* been hers.

But today, like every day before, he'd left to go to work. Max was who he was, and he was unwavering in his quest to save the world, one case at a time. She and Max Jr. were just two people in a country of millions, and her ex-husband had been purposed with protecting the masses.

Allie had realized, too late, that she'd been selfish to expect more from him. He'd made it clear when they met that his life wasn't his own. His time and attention weren't his to give freely. He had a gift and a calling. And they weren't to her.

She forced away the hollow feeling that always accompanied those thoughts, and tidied the house with increased fervor. Most of the decor at her new place had once been at their shared home in Traverse City, but she'd taken everything when she'd left. Max had insisted on it. While it'd hurt her to think he didn't want anything from their life together, Max had been convinced the move would be easier on their son this way. He'd thought Max Jr. should be surrounded by as many familiar things as possible.

That was one more thing about her ex-husband. He wasn't greedy. Wasn't cruel or jealous, inconsiderate or needy. Max was honorable and compassionate, fair and unwavering. He was everything she'd ever wanted in a partner and more, but he was also something she couldn't have anticipated and wasn't ready to accept. Max was already spoken for. Already wholly committed to the US government and general population.

The oven dinged, turning her toward the kitchen. Max Jr. would be up from his nap soon, and Allie had plenty to do before kissing his precious cherub face again.

She'd prepared Max's favorite meal in anticipation of his arrival, and she'd enjoyed every minute of it. Allie loved to cook, but she hadn't had cause to prepare anything more significant than a variety of soups, sandwiches and salads since moving to Grand Rapids. Cooking for one was borderline depressing, so she'd eaten at her parents' house more often than not. Once Max Jr. had a few more teeth, she planned to revisit some of her old favorites in the kitchen.

For now, she concentrated on the baked ziti assembled in her favorite glass baking dish. She'd already boiled the pasta and browned the ground beef, then layered them with tomato sauce, Parmesan and shredded mozzarella cheese. She slid the dish into the oven to warm up and melt the cheese and set the timer, then sliced a loaf of bread from the local bakery and loaded it with butter and garlic. The bread would go in after the ziti came out.

Allie took a long breath and centered herself. Max had never come for dinner at her new home, but he was coming tonight.

The doorbell rang, and her heart leaped. "He's here," she whispered. "Be cool."

She peeked outside before opening the door, a

habit Max had instilled in her when they were dating and insisted upon until it had become second nature.

He caught her gazing through the window and smiled.

"Come in," she said, pulling the door wide and hurrying him inside. "It's freezing out there. How are you? I'm glad you're here." She bit her lip to keep from rambling. "Good day?"

Max watched her for a long beat, humor twisting his lips and something more intense flashing in his eyes. "I'm doing better now. Thanks for the invitation."

She nodded. "Dinner's in the oven. Can I get you something to drink while it bakes?" She frowned. "I didn't think to ask if you have to go out again tonight. I could've had everything ready when you got here." It wasn't uncommon for Max to be called away at any moment, but it was also highly unusual for him to be on time. "Are you on a dinner break?"

"Unless there's a major change in the case, or another bombing—" he grimaced "—I don't have to leave until morning." He grinned. "You know what I mean."

Allie felt her smile rise. "Make yourself comfortable. I'll pour some coffee." She knew Max liked a good cup more than a cocktail or wine, and she'd bought a specialty blend earlier just for his visit.

She kept an eye on him as he made a loop through the living room. The adjoining kitchen was separated by only a small island, allowing her to watch and evaluate his reaction to her home. Each time they'd gotten together for his visitation with Max Jr., Allie had met him somewhere between the two homes, to save him the added travel time.

She filled a pair of mugs with coffee while Max admired new photos of their son, then paused before a wall of framed images. Including many of himself.

Allie had created a gallery collection along the far wall. Max in his military dress uniform. Max in fatigues. Max kissing her at their wedding ceremony. Max holding their newborn at the hospital. And Max with the TCD. She'd included plenty of framed selfies from their little family's early days, and images of Max Jr. as he grew. "I thought it was important for Max Jr. to see you every day," she said, heading back to the living room with a mug of coffee in each hand. "And to see we were happy once. A subtle reminder that he was made with love."

Max accepted the mug, brows furrowed, scrutinizing. His specialty. "I didn't realize you still had these photos of me in the military. Or of me and the TCD."

"We're proud of you," she said. "Of who you are and what you do. Whatever else happens in your life or ours, Max Jr. and I are always proud. Keeping the pictures on display is like having a piece of you here, even when the rest of you can't be." Kind of like Max's suggestion she keep all of their things in the divorce. "Consistency is key."

Max watched her, probably seeing through the forced nonchalance. Probably sensing her desire to reach for him. To tell him she loved him despite everything, and that she always would. Hopefully, not reading her more private thoughts about some of the things she missed the most.

"I'm sorry," he said suddenly, his eyes searching hers. "I realized a while ago that I never said that, and I should have."

Allie's breath caught. Her heart thundered. "Yeah?"

He dipped his chin infinitesimally. "I let you down. You and I were a team, and I dropped the ball when it counted. You deserved more. I'm sorry."

She opened her mouth to tell him it was okay, everything worked out, or something equally encouraging, but that wasn't true. And she and Max never lied to one another. "Thank you."

His deep brown eyes crinkled at the sides in warmth and acceptance. "That was easy."

She shrugged. "It means a lot to hear you say, and I appreciate it."

His dead-sexy smile spread, and she felt her bones begin to melt.

A small coo rose through the speaker of the baby monitor on the coffee table, breaking the mood and sending Allie back a step.

"May I?" Max asked, already moving toward the hallway to the bedrooms. He paused at the edge of the room, awaiting her permission.

She nodded. "Sure. First door on the left. Thanks."

Allie escaped to the kitchen and traded her coffee for a glass of iced water, then moved the baked ziti to the countertop before sliding the bread into the oven.

"There's my little man," Max said. His voice echoed through the monitor on the coffee table.

Max Jr. babbled and laughed. "Dada."

Allie froze. Her heart swelled, and her eyes stung unexpectedly. She shut the oven door and inched toward the monitor. Max Jr. had been calling her and both her parents Dada for days, but it was the first time Max had heard it.

"Dada," their toddler repeated. "Dada. Dada."

"That's right," Max said, his voice full of awe and gravel. "I'm your daddy, and I've missed you so much."

Allie drifted to the living room, eyes glued on the little monitor, its lights dancing with every sound in the nursery. Grainy images of Max and their son filled the tiny screen. She lifted the device and pressed it to her chest, savoring the moment.

"I hope you've been taking good care of your mama," Max said. "She's tough, but that doesn't mean she can't use some help from time to time. Like, maybe, after your naps, you can clean up around here. Do your laundry or grab the car keys and bring home the groceries."

Allie smiled, and a tear slid over her cheek as Max changed Max Jr.'s diaper, narrating the process in a silly voice. The idea her little boy would ever be old enough to borrow the car was both surreal and bittersweet. The idea Max wouldn't be at her side to worry until their baby got back safely was just sad.

The sound of Max's footfalls echoed in the short hall, and she set the monitor aside. She returned to the kitchen, then filled her son's lidded cup with milk. Hopefully he liked ziti as much as his father; otherwise, it would be peanut butter and jelly for Max Jr. tonight. Probably with vanilla yogurt and sliced strawberries on the side.

Max appeared as she ferried the glass baking dish to the trivet on the table. "Something smells like heaven."

"Garlic bread," she said, turning back to the oven. "And baked ziti." She stole a look over her shoulder, watching as Max strapped their son into his high chair, then dropped a kiss on his head.

Max Jr. grabbed the sippy cup she'd placed on his tray and began to drink immediately while Max stroked their son's generous curls. Their baby was perfect and beautiful, an image of Allie and Max combined. Light brown skin and hazel eyes, the sweetest loose brown curls, and a smile to light up any room.

Allie fought the urge to cry tears of contentment and joy. If only this could be her reality every night.

Chapter Eight

Max collected the plates stacked beside the sink, then set the table while Allie tossed a salad and cut some ziti into small pieces for Max Jr. It was nice moving around the kitchen with her like old times. They'd always had such an effortless flow together, and he'd missed it more than he'd realized. He tried not to read into the fact she'd made his favorite meal, but it was nice that she remembered. Or maybe she made baked ziti every night these days. He couldn't be sure.

Still, what if she'd looked forward to this all day, too? He'd practically run to the hotel to wash up and change before coming over. Axel, always his roommate on trips like these, had taunted him mercilessly for his nerves. Then Max had circled the block twice, killing time so he wouldn't arrive too early or rush her.

Now that he was here, with her and Max Jr., he wasn't sure how he'd be able to leave. He didn't expect to go to work tonight, so the visit wouldn't have to be rushed, but no amount of time would be enough to make the goodbye any easier. Max Jr. had grown so much since he'd last seen him. His little face had changed, filled out and matured. He was no longer a baby. Max Jr. was a toddler, and he could say *dada*. Max's heart gave a heavy thump at the memory. Thankfully, his son hadn't forgotten him. But how long would it be before he did?

"Everything okay?" Allie asked, taking a seat at the head of the table and dropping a napkin onto her lap.

"Perfect," he said. "Thank you for inviting me and for cooking. I'd reciprocate if I could."

She nodded. "Anytime, Max."

If only he really could reciprocate. But that time had passed. He'd blown his chance with Allie, and the devastation returned to him full force. It'd taken months of burying himself in his work to get past it the first time. To convince himself not to call her when he'd had a hard day or heard their wedding song on the radio.

"So how's it going?" she asked. "With the case. A productive first day?"

Max cleared his throat and lowered into the seat to her right. "Actually, yes," he said, trying not to stare too long or hard at her soft curls, full lips or flushed skin. "I'm not one hundred percent certain, but my gut says we've identified the bomber. And I think he's the man you described seeing on the night of the Burger Mania explosion." He shifted to slide his phone from the pocket of his jeans, then accessed the image provided by Jordyn's roommate. "Does he look familiar?"

Allie took the phone and examined the image. "I think that's him." Her hazel eyes widened as she pulled her gaze from the phone to Max, then back. "Same coat. The hair looks right. The beard. I didn't get a great look at his face last night, but the posture and everything else feels like the guy I saw."

Max set the phone on the table. "He's our prime suspect. We haven't been able to find him for questioning, but I think you should see that sketch artist as soon as possible."

"I met with a sketch artist this afternoon. The image was being finalized when I headed home to make dinner," she said, eyebrows rising. "I was glad to help, but your gut is rarely wrong." Allie had always said his instincts were the reason she didn't worry as much as someone else in her position might have. She trusted him and respected what he did. "Who is he?"

"Fritz O'Lear. He was a real-estate agent at the Ramsey Realty office for a while, then left a few months back, frustrated over his poor performance and taunted by a fellow Realtor for low sales numbers. He was rejected twice by a young Burger Mania employee he made uncomfortable, then asked out on a date. The girl and the Realtor who'd given him the hardest time were both casualties."

"Sounds like your guy," Allie said. "Have you found any other possible suspects?"

"Not yet, but Opaline vowed to dig back to pre-school if needed." He smiled unintentionally.

Allie joined him. "Opaline isn't to be trifled with. She'll probably come back with his elementary school report cards and Little League photos."

Max laughed, both proud of his coworker and incredibly thankful she didn't have reason to dig into him.

"How is Opaline?" Allie asked. "I always liked her. She's so positive and congenial."

"She hasn't changed, still all sunshine until her sister speaks." That little mystery had been a topic of more than one conversation between Max and Allie. An unsolved mystery he was glad to leave alone since the women were both his teammates, and it wasn't wise to know more than any of them wanted.

"I hope they get that worked out soon."

Max Jr. shoved bits of pasta into his mouth with both fists, his spoon already tossed aside.

Allie wiped his sauce-covered cheeks and fingers with her napkin and gave him an adoring smile. "Do you think this Fritz O'Lear is on the run or plotting another attack?"

Max forked another bite of homemade heaven, inhaling the tangy scent of tomato sauce and the rich, salty aroma of melted cheese. "I've been asking myself the same question all day."

She seemed to consider his answer. "The man I saw was completely unfazed by the fire, the screams, the plume of ghastly smoke." Allie wet her lips and glanced at Max Jr., then leaned in Max's direction. "I think he liked what he saw."

Max stilled. He'd always appreciated Allie's interest in his cases. She was incredibly insightful, and sometimes riffing theories with her was more productive than the work he did with his team. Something about a change of setting, maybe. But he suspected it was Allie's ability to ask the right questions and ferret out the thoughts he sometimes lost in the deluge of information.

Allie had once dreamed of being an investigative reporter, but she'd given that up long before he'd met her. And as much as Allie clearly still enjoyed working the puzzle pieces of an investigation into one neatly defined picture, he knew she'd never take any unnecessary risk now. Not with Max Jr. relying on her, and Max respected that.

"I'm afraid you're right," Max admitted. "He fits the profile of someone who's been rejected and pushed around long enough to have a lengthy list of perceived offenders. And clearly he's snapped. He might plan on punishing a lot more people."

"You always say bombers are in it for the power and control."

"Something they've usually never had," he said.

Allie frowned. "Power is intoxicating, especially to an underdog."

Max nodded. She was absolutely right. And when the underdog came unhinged, their power became incredibly dangerous.

"What's on the agenda for tomorrow?" Allie asked. "Anything I can do to help?"

"No. Meeting with the sketch artist was great. Now I just need you and Max Jr. to lie low and stay safe. The TCD is waiting for more information from Opaline. Until then, we'll keep working any leads we can get. No one we've spoken to had a personal connection to O'Lear, so we're running blind. We've been to his home and both crime scenes, so we've lost the element of surprise."

Allie cringed. "If he thinks you're closing in on him, he'll work faster or retaliate. They always go full bananas when they feel cornered."

He set his fork beside the freshly emptied plate and wiped his mouth with a napkin, utterly content. "Right again." Inwardly, he smiled, warmed by the idea that Allie was acting as if she were part of the team, trying to help out.

"Any idea who the next target could be? Maybe your team can offer them protection while you hunt the bomber."

Max grinned.

"What?" Allie's cheeks reddened.

"You've got a big heart, and you would've made a hell of a reporter."

She pushed a bite of pasta into her mouth and dragged her attention back to their son. "Thanks."

The evening passed in a blur. Hours were gone in minutes, and Max carried his sleeping son to bed at ten, limp and drooling in his arms. He stroked Max Jr.'s piles of sweet-scented curls and wished for more nights like tonight. Then he returned to Allie in the living room.

Max hadn't fought her when she'd served the divorce papers, because he'd known she was right. She and Max Jr. deserved more than a part-time husband and father. They'd argued about it—a lot—leading up to her giving him an ultimatum. His job or his family. He'd put off that decision so long that she filled in the blank herself. He chose the job. It hadn't felt like a conscious choice at the time. He'd known he was needed at the FBI and by the TCD. His happiness had been a necessary sacrifice for the number of lives he'd saved since then.

Funny how he'd once thought losing his leg was the worst thing he'd ever go through.

She leaned against the doorway, watching as he returned. "I'm glad you came tonight."

"Me, too." He smiled.

"Good." She cast a pointed gaze at the clock. "I'm guessing you have an early day tomorrow."

"I do." And he knew that raising Max Jr. on her own meant that she would have to rise early, too. "I should probably get going." He threaded his arms into the sleeves of a well-worn leather bomber and tugged a knit cap over his head. "Can I see you tomorrow?"

Allie's mouth opened, then shut. A smile spread, and she nodded. "We'd like that."

"Then I'll be here. I'll call if anything comes up, or if I'm running late." He reached for the door when she didn't move to let him out.

"Wait." She wet her lips and searched his eyes. "Stay," she said softly. Her shoulders tensed, and a measure of worry clouded her eyes. "Don't go."

"What?" He felt his brows furrow as confusion and hope battled in his heart. "You want me to stay. Here?"

"It makes sense," she said, pursing her pretty red lips and crossing her arms. "Why go to a hotel when you can stay here? You'll get extra time with Max Jr. before you have to leave town. The food is definitely better than whatever they're serving at the hotel café, and the company's not bad. I can make up the couch for you. I know you have a go bag in your truck with at least two days' worth of work clothes."

Max's eyes never left hers as he stripped out of his coat and pulled off his hat, then set the pair gently on the arm of the nearby couch. A strange tension formed in his core.

Allie stepped forward slowly, only breaking their locked gaze when she wrapped her arms around his torso and pressed her cheek to his chest.

He curved protective arms around her, exactly where they belonged, and he breathed in the scent of her skin, perfume and hair. He savored her warmth and the rhythm of her heartbeat against his core. "How about I make breakfast for us tomorrow? A thank-you for the delicious dinner and use of your couch."

She laughed. "Deal. Max Jr. loves scrambled eggs. Lots of cheese. I prefer veggies."

"Done."

Her eyes were glossed with unshed tears as she released him. "I'll get some blankets and pillows for the couch."

She hurried away, and Max stared after her.

The tension he'd noted in his core suddenly began to feel a lot like hope. For what, he wasn't sure, but it'd been a long time since he'd had any hope, and he planned to hold on to it as long as he could.

Chapter Nine

Allie woke to the sound of her alarm for the first time in two years. She hadn't slept especially well during her pregnancy or any night since, and the sensation of waking without Max Jr.'s help was slightly disconcerting. She stopped the alarm, waiting for her son to call out, but there was a distinct silence in her home, save for some shuffling from the living room.

The previous day rushed back with an adrenaline slap. Max was in town. In her home. Right down the hall.

She jerked upright, then darted out of bed and raced for the shower. Thirty harried minutes later, she was as fresh and calm as possible, given the fact she was about to see Max again.

Allie padded barefoot toward the kitchen, following the delightful sounds of her baby's laughter and inhaling the rich, cheesy scent of scrambled eggs and her blessed morning coffee. Max came slowly into view around the corner, their son on one hip as he danced and sang to "Purple Rain" by Prince.

His strong, protective arms held him tight as they dipped and turned. Black pants accentuated Max's fit physique. His gray sweater clung to the toned curves of his chest and biceps.

His phone was plugged into her dock on the counter, a familiar playlist lifting from its speaker. The baby monitor was dark, powered off, beside the dock.

Max Jr. laughed and smacked his daddy's chest with chubby, gleeful palms.

Max caught hers a moment later, not at all surprised by her presence. "Good morning." His gaze traveled slowly over her, steadily raising her temperature. "This guy gets up almost as early as his daddy."

She shuffled forward, making a memory of the scene before her, not realizing how many similar moments she'd too easily forgotten. "Don't pretend you slept."

"What?" Max asked. "Just because I'm at least a foot longer than that couch?"

She crossed her arms and leaned a hip against the counter. "Because you don't sleep. We haven't been apart so long that I've forgotten how you are while on a case." Allie peeked over her shoulder, into the living area behind her.

Max had folded up the blankets and stacked his pillow neatly on top, but a coffee mug, two empty water bottles and a stack of papers cluttered the coffee table beside his open laptop. He must've brought that in from his SUV after she went to bed, along with the change of clothes he was wearing and his toiletries. There was no denying he'd had a shower, or that he'd used his favorite soaps and cologne. Both scents were far more delicious-smelling than anything on the stovetop.

Max carried their son to his high chair and strapped him securely in, then went to plate the eggs he'd scrambled. "I stayed in touch with the team in case of new developments."

"Trying to locate Fritz O'Lear and determine his next target?" she guessed, moving into the kitchen.

"That's about it." Max smiled.

Allie kissed Max Jr.'s chubby cheeks and stroked his soft curls. Then she poured a mug of coffee from the fresh pot. "Any luck?"

"No, but I'm more familiar with the case now. A very good thing," Max said.

Allie agreed. "Everything smells amazing," she said. "Thank you for this. Max Jr. and I usually just have fruit and cereal."

Max ferried their plates to the table, setting his and Allie's across from one another, with Max Jr.'s in between.

Allie watched her ex-husband closely, missing him and mornings like these more than she'd realized. "How are you holding up with this case?" she asked. "You don't get a lot of bombers. And I mean you personally, not the team—how are you really doing?"

Max's gaze flicked to her. He sat straighter, forearms on the table. "You're the only one who's asked that."

"Everyone else is wondering," she said. "They don't want to be rude or overstep."

"Not you," he said, expression blank but searching.

"No. Not me." Allie softened her tone, not wanting to push Max, but needing him to understand he mattered. Not just his physical safety, but his feelings, too. His mental and emotional health were important and valuable. Max was more than a conduit or tool to reach an objective. He was human. And he'd once been her human. "I'm more concerned about how you're doing than my manners. You're dealing with memories your team members aren't, and you're carrying a burden they don't understand. I want to know you're okay."

"I'm okay."

She smiled. "Just like that?" she asked. "It's not a sign of weakness to admit this is hard for you, Max."

His jaw set. "It's my job to carry on without letting my feelings get in the way."

She would've laughed if it wasn't so heartbreaking. He'd been on a case when she'd served him with divorce papers. She hadn't planned that, but the TCD went where it was needed, when it was needed. Max included. He'd stayed the course. Caught the bad guy, then moved out after he'd come home. "No, I guess you don't."

"That's not what I meant."

"I know," she said. "It's okay." She lifted her fork

and ate every bite of her eggs without another word. Determined to keep her tongue busy before she said something she'd regret.

She and Max were lucky to have an amicable divorce. Most people only dreamed of a relationship as civil as theirs eight months out. "I just want you to be happy, healthy and cared for," she said, the minute her breakfast was gone. "You spend all your time caring for others. Someone has to make sure you're also taking care of you."

His sour expression loosened. "I'm okay, Allie." He reached for her hand across the table, then curled his fingers around hers. "This is my job, and I'm good at it. I'm probably feeling all the ways you think I am, but I don't want to talk about it."

One more thing that hadn't changed. Max had always told her his pain kept him vigilant.

His phone buzzed, and he released her to retrieve it from his pocket.

Allie recognized Axel's face as Max swiped the screen to life. "Go on. Take the call. I'll clean up."

Max ducked into the living room, tidying the coffee table as he spoke with his friend and supervisor.

Allie cleared the breakfast table, then refilled her coffee while she waited.

When Max returned, his expression was one of regret and anticipation. "I have to go."

She unfastened Max Jr. from the high chair and passed him to Max for a kiss, then hugged him against her hip when Max returned him. "We'll walk you to the door."

Max donned his coat and hat, then paused to look at Allie and Max Jr.

The familiar tug of hope and fear churned in her core. "Be safe."

"Always." He leaned in to kiss their son once more, then stroked Allie's cheek. "Please stay home from the mall today. We don't know who else could be on this guy's hit list, and there are a lot of people working where you do. Any one of them could be a target, which would put you in danger. I can't live with that."

Allie pressed her lips tight, aching to heed his warning, without behaving too rashly. Grand Rapids was a big town, and there was no reason to assume the mall would ever become a target, let alone the specific area near her kiosk. "I can work on custom orders and invoicing from home, but when that's all caught up, I have to make new sales if I'm going to stay afloat. I can't stay here indefinitely."

"Give me seventy-two hours," he said. "Or as much time as you can. That's all I'm asking."

"I'll try."

A slow smile of satisfaction spread across his face. "See you again tonight."

She smiled. "I'll cook. All you have to do is show up, preferably uninjured." She set a palm against his strong jaw and rose onto her toes, then pressed a kiss to his cheek.

Max lifted her hand from his cheek and pressed a kiss against her fingertips. "See you tonight."

MAX'S HEART BEAT hard and fast as he drove away from Allie's house, heading back to the TCD's temporary headquarters at the Grand Rapids Police Department. Axel had called the team together for a morning meeting, and Max didn't want to miss anything. He clutched the wheel and concentrated on the roads as he pressed the gas pedal with more purpose, images of his perfect little boy and beautiful ex-wife flashing warmly in his mind. He needed to locate and apprehend Fritz O'Lear before he hurt anyone else. *Before he injures or kills someone else's child or loved one.*

The woman at the police department desk buzzed Max through the locked security door before he had a chance to stop and raise his badge.

Most of the team was already in place as he entered the conference room. Anticipation was palpable in the air.

Axel met Max at the front of the long table, dressed in a gray suit and holding a massive disposable cup of coffee. "How was breakfast?"

"Excellent. I made it." Max fought a smile. He'd told Axel he was staying at Allie's last night when Axel texted, wanting to meet him at the hotel bar. The confession had resulted in a long, slow whistle from Axel.

Axel waited for additional information. He raised the giant cup to his lips when the details didn't come. "So you'll be back at the hotel tonight?"

Max's traitorous lips twitched. "No."

He stepped around Axel, then took a seat.

Axel narrowed his eyes. "Interesting." He lowered into the chair across from Max, keeping close watch on his friend.

Max frowned at Axel's summarization. "It's definitely that."

There had been moments this morning when he'd felt certain there was something more still there between Allie and him, but he couldn't be sure or allow himself to dwell. Not now. Not when there was a bomber on the loose, and Max needed his head in the game.

The remaining members of their team filtered in, filling the last few chairs around the table.

Rihanna pulled the door shut behind them. "Good morning. Glad to see everyone's here." She lifted a remote and pointed it at the large projector screen. "Let's go ahead and get started."

The screen lit, and Opaline appeared. She waved and smiled. Her hot-pink lips parted, exposing a wide set of perfect white teeth. "Hello! Good morning," she said. "I hope some of you managed to get a little sleep last night. I didn't." She laughed, then lifted a bowl-sized coffee mug into view. "How about we recap before moving forward? You guys first."

The team members took turns sharing theories and tidbits they'd unearthed about the victims' lives.

Selena took the initiative to sum up the offerings. "So I think we were on the right track yesterday, by assuming this is a vengeance mission. He's targeting people he thinks did him wrong."

Carly tapped her pen against her chin, nodding as Selena spoke. She turned her attention to the team when Selena finished. "I've seen this pattern of behavior a lot. It's a top motivator in cases involving poison. On the surface, poisonings and bombings seem incredibly different, but their perpetrators are often very similar. In both types of crimes, the killer often sees him- or herself as an underdog. They make a deadly power play from a distance that keeps them safe."

"Agreed," Opaline said, pointing a lime-green fingernail at the camera. "Good. I love it when we're single-minded." She clicked her mouse a few times, then looked back at the camera. "I was able to dig up some details on Fritz O'Lear."

The team shifted, collectively, eager for whatever she'd unearthed. According to their shared thoughts and input, none of them had had any more luck than Max last night.

Opaline smiled, and the team's phones began to buzz. "I just sent you everything I have. It's not a lot, but it's more than we had last night, and I'm confident there will be more to come as this day moves forward. These details have been brought to you by a steady stream of energy drinks and the legendary Lopez tenacity."

Max opened the message and read the brief bullet-point list. Distant family members. Hobbies, including bowling and billiards. "This is a good start, Opaline."

He stood to address the table, unable to be still

any longer. "Let's break this list down, split up and move out. We need photos of O'Lear posted at every local pool hall and bowling alley. We'll reach out to the distant family members and try to come away with more leads from each stop. Someone knows where this guy is, and we need to find him. Today."

Chapter Ten

Max followed Axel up the cracked walkway to Fritz O'Lear's building once more. Again the neighborhood was quiet, everyone likely kept inside by the cold. "If he doesn't answer this time, let's knock on some other doors. See what the neighbors think of him." And maybe enlist the local PD in surveilling the man's home until he showed up.

Axel stopped on the small stoop and waved to a man, visible through the cruddy double-paned security window. "Agreed."

Hopefully, the residents would talk. Convincing neighbors, family or friends to share information with law enforcement wasn't always as easy as it should be, and even when people opened up, there was the matter of confirming their tales. Some people were honest and helpful, but others held back for a variety of reasons. Fear of retaliation by the criminal in question or of being flagged as a narc were common holdups, as well as an unfortunate and misguided distrust of officials.

Feelings of allegiance to the suspect were the

toughest to get past. It was sometimes hard to convince a friend or family member that their loved one could've been involved in any illegal activity. And on the flip side, there were folks who knew absolutely nothing about the person or problem at hand but intentionally tied up the investigation with all sorts of unfounded stories and blatant lies. Some of those folks were bored, lonely and desperate for the attention. Others were simply troublemakers.

The old man inside the building inched closer to the window, peering back at the agents. Confusion crumbled his bushy salt-and-pepper brows. "Who are you? What do you want?" he asked through the door.

Axel raised his badge. "FBI."

The man squinted at the badge, then swung his attention from Axel to Max. He seemed to weigh his options before deciding to do the right thing.

The door clicked open, and the man cocked his head. "Is that thing real?"

"Yes." Axel stepped forward, pushing his way inside.

The man fumbled to get out of the way, eyes wide. "What's going on?" His hands were full of envelopes and flyers. One of the doors in the bank of mailboxes was open. He hurried around to close and lock it.

Max did his best to look authoritative without intimidating the older gentleman. "Thanks for letting us in. It's getting cold out there."

"What's this about?" the man asked. "What happened?"

"We're Special Agents Morrow and McRay," Axel explained, tapping his chest, then pointing to Max. "Have you lived here long?"

The man furrowed his bushy brows. "Seven years in September."

"Do you know many of the people in this building?" Max asked.

"Most." He fixed his appraising gaze on Max. "Almost everyone by face, if not by name." He clutched his mail protectively against a baggy Mr. Rogers–style cardigan. Khaki pants hung askew on his slight frame, and Max wondered if the man had lost weight or been given the too-large clothes. He hated the thought of his father or grandfather living in a run-down building like this one.

"I'm Max." He offered the man a hand. "You live here with your family?"

"No. They're all gone now. My Ellie passed in February '03. Kids are grown, living all around the country. No one's in Michigan. Everyone's busy. I'm Henry."

Max smiled. "Nice to meet you, Henry."

He pushed heavy-framed glasses up his narrow nose, magnifying milky blue eyes. "Is someone here in trouble? Or are they on the run?"

"Maybe neither," Max said.

Henry made a derisive sound. "The government doesn't send two big hulks like you out to look for someone who's not in trouble or on the run."

Max grinned despite himself. Neither he nor Axel was considered especially large in their circle, but compared to the man before them, reaching for five-eight, Henry's assessment was one he couldn't argue with. "Do you know the man in apartment 325?"

"O'Lear," Henry said, looking proud.

"That's right. You know Mr. O'Lear?" Max asked, pulling his phone from an interior coat pocket.

"No." Henry pointed to the mailboxes, each with a different last name.

Axel smiled.

Max brought up the photo of O'Lear from the real-estate ad. "Is this him?"

Henry squinted and stared. "Maybe, but he doesn't look like that now, if it's the guy I'm thinking of."

Max flipped to the grainier, more distant shot of O'Lear leaving Burger Mania. "How about him?"

"That's the guy," Henry said, raising his eyes to meet Max's. "He looks like that now. I never saw him looking the other way, like a shiny penny. Like you two. I'd remember."

Max laughed. He'd been called a lot of things, never shiny or a penny.

Axel craned his head for a pointed look up the staircase. "Is Mr. O'Lear home now? Any chance you've seen him today?"

"No. Come to think about it, I haven't seen him since he had that argument with the super." Henry rubbed his chin and jawline. "That's been a day or two. I can't be sure. Sometimes I get fuzzy when it comes to time."

The sound of an old-fashioned telephone interrupted, and Henry pulled a large flip phone from his pocket. He frowned at the number on the screen. "Speaking of losing time. This is my doctor's office. If I miss another appointment, they're going to charge me for not canceling." He raised the phone to his ear and wrinkled his nose.

"Thanks, Henry." Axel moved toward the stairs. "I'm going to take a look. Maybe you missed him."

"Hello?" Henry answered the call.

Max handed Henry a business card. "Thank you for your time," he said quietly. "If you need anything else, or think of something you want to tell us, call."

Max followed Axel to apartment 325 and waited while he knocked. As predicted, no answer.

They parted ways from there. Axel moved to the next door. Max went to the second floor. More than an hour later, they were back at the first-floor mailboxes, with Henry in tow. Max had unintentionally brought him out again by knocking on his apartment door. From there, Henry made introductions. He started with his name and apartment number, then introduced Max. The residents were chattier and visibly more at ease with Henry's company than when Max had knocked alone, so he kept him on the case.

"Anything?" Axel asked, already waiting for Max.

"Not really." Max rested his hands on his hips. "Of the people who answered, and admitted to recognizing O'Lear's name or photo, all I learned was that he was quiet. Kept to himself."

Axel nodded. "Same here. Most folks didn't want

to talk, but the ones who did all said he seemed like a nice guy."

Henry stood taller. "You should've had me come along on all the interviews. Folks liked talking to me, and you know, that's what they say about the serial killers. They all seemed like nice guys."

Axel dragged his gaze from Henry to Max. "You took him on the interviews?"

Max smiled.

"Is he a serial killer?" Henry pressed. "I hope not. That guy had a temper."

Max took a beat to process the information. "He was arguing with your building superintendent the last time you saw him?"

Henry nodded. "Yeah. Right out here by the mailboxes."

"What were they fighting about?"

Henry rubbed a soft wrinkled finger against his brow. "Rent, I think. He was late on payment for the month, and the super doesn't have a grace period. He's a real pain. He doesn't want to fix anything around here, but he threatens to kick us out if we're a little short or a couple days late."

"O'Lear's been out of work," Axel said, catching Max's attention over Henry's head. "Probably running through his savings, assuming he had any."

Henry left his eyebrow alone and snapped his finger. "He said he should get a break on rent because his thermostat is broken. I remember now. There aren't any breaks on rent, and I haven't seen him moving, so I figured he's staying somewhere else 'cause it's so darn cold."

Snow had begun to fall in fat, steady flakes outside the filthy security window. Wind whipped through barren limbs and bent saplings in a park across the street. It wasn't a good time for a broken thermostat.

"How long has O'Lear lived here?" Axel asked, drawing Max's attention back inside.

Henry shrugged. "Six, eight months? You sure he's not a serial killer? You guys only come out for serious stuff. Is he a fugitive? Is that your shtick?"

"No. That's the US Marshals," Axel said, sliding his eyes to Max, lips twitching with suppressed humor.

"Well, it's not as if this guy is wanted for robbing a bank," Henry said. "Anyone with money wouldn't stay here. So what is it?" He scowled and pressed a palm to his chest. "Is he a pedophile? We've got kids in this building. That isn't it, is it? He's a pedophile?"

"Not that we know of," Max said. "We think he might know something about the bombs that have detonated in Grand Rapids this week."

Henry cringed. "That's better than a pedophile. But if you're right, I'd hate to be our super." He turned his eyes to the door at the end of the hall marked 101 and also Staff.

The only door neither Max nor Axel had knocked on yet.

"Is that your superintendent's office?" Axel asked.

"Yeah, and it's his apartment, too. He has an office inside the door. Then his apartment is through another door in the office. We take our rent to him in there. He owns the building, so don't let that sign fool you. We don't have any staff."

Max strode in the door's direction, instinct propelling him across the threadbare carpets. He pounded on the door.

"He's not there," Henry said. "I saw him go out after you guys headed upstairs. He goes out every day around now, and he's gone until noon. He comes back with takeout. Then he spends the rest of his day avoiding unhappy tenants."

Axel swore under his breath. He dragged a hand through his hair, then locked gazes with Max. "I'm going to call this in. Reach out to the team. We'll stake out the building."

"Henry?" Max asked. "Will you call me when the superintendent gets back?"

"Sure." Henry patted the chest pocket of his sweater, where the top of Max's business card poked out. "I'll call you if I see the other guy, too. O'Lear. Apartment 325."

"Don't approach him," Max said. "Just let us know he's home."

Henry nodded, the color and bravado bleeding from his face. "Will do."

Max and Axel headed back to the SUV, heads down against the biting wind. Inside, and engine running, Axel adjusted the heaters, and the men sent texts with their new information to the team.

Axel's phone rang a moment later, Aria's face centering the screen. "Morrow," he said, answering the call on speaker and holding the phone in Max's direction. "I'm here with Max. What do you have?"

"I'm thinking about timing," Selena said, forgoing small talk and customary greetings. She was using Aria's phone. "Ramsey Realty was hit four days ago. Burger Mania two days ago. One day in between each. To recover. Recuperate. Gather additional materials," she rattled, "maybe just to gloat and enjoy the press coverage."

Aria's voice echoed from the background. "Bomb day. Off day. Bomb day. Off day. You know what that makes today?"

"A bomb day." The women's voices arrived in near unison.

Max's muscles tightened, and tension coiled uncomfortably in his core. "O'Lear hasn't been back here since he argued with the superintendent."

"Could he be planning to bomb the building?" Selena asked.

Max stared through the icy winter day outside his window. He'd hoped O'Lear had chosen the previous bombing times to limit collateral damage. Just after 7:00 a.m. at the realty office. After 2:00 a.m. at Burger Mania. But what if he was wrong? What if O'Lear's only consideration had been the assurance he would get his target? If he wasn't concerned about the number of additional casualties, then the entire apartment building could be in danger. "The superintendent isn't there right now," he said, turning back to Axel and the phone in his partner's hand. Determination powered his words, and a plan formed in his head. "That buys us some time, but we're going to have to move."

"I'll rally the team," Aria said. "Selena's reaching out to Carly and Rihanna now. We can be there in fifteen."

Max brought up the dial pad on his phone. "I'll get local PD out here along with the bomb squad. Contact Fire and Rescue."

"You've got it," Aria said.

"I'll sweep the building with Sergeant Sims and hope we're wrong."

"And not too late," Axel said. "It's already after ten, and according to Henry, the super gets back predictably at noon. A prime time for detonation."

AN HOUR LATER, the Grand Rapids police had located the building superintendent, William Teske, and moved him to a safe location while Max, the TCD team, first responders and the bomb squad set up outside the building in preparation for the worst.

Residents had been moved to an off-site location with plenty of heat and donated meals from a nearby café while they waited to hear if their homes blew up. Pets were caged and would be sheltered by the local animal protection organization until the building was deemed safe for everyone's return.

Overall, Max was impressed with the cooperation and efficiency of so many local agencies toward a common goal.

He was less impressed, though not at all surprised, however, by the local media's massive response. Once they'd gotten wind of the evacuation, they'd shown up in droves. News vans from all around the county had begun to arrive as residents and pets were relocated, and the reporters continually encroached on the perimeter Max had set.

Now onlookers lined streets and corners, drawn from their homes by Breaking News announcements on their televisions, radios and web browsers. Officers worked to keep everyone back, but there wasn't enough crime-scene tape in Michigan to rope off a radius as large as Max would've preferred.

Snow continued to fall, coating roads, grass and walkways as Max worked out his game plan. Flakes piled on his teammates' hats and the shoulders of their coats, no longer melting immediately from their body heat. Their cheeks were pink from the biting wind, their gloved hands shoved deep into pockets or wrapped around fast-cooling cups of tea or coffee.

The city's engineering department had provided digital blueprints of the tenement building, giving the TCD an insider's look at the bones of the structure. There were only one or two places a bomb the size of those used in the Ramsey Realty and Burger Mania attacks could be placed to maximize damage to Teske's apartment, so those would be checked first. From there, Max would widen the search range for due diligence, viewing every location where O'Lear could have planned to reach his target.

He donned his protective gear on autopilot, fighting memories of the last time he'd geared up as a US soldier, searching for a potential bomb. The EOD—Explosive Ordnance Disposal—suit was heavy, at least sixty pounds, and unbearably hot, worse in a desert region already burning at well over one hundred degrees. Images of that day returned, and his heart rate rose. Heat licked up his neck and across his cheeks despite the current icy winds.

"How you doing?" Axel asked, breaking away from the team to check on Max. The hem of his wool coat flapped in the breeze. "Need any help?"

"Nah," Max said, fastening the final strips of Velcro at his wrists and willing the panic to recede. "I'm good."

"You look flushed," Axel said. "Can I get you anything? Water?"

Max nodded. "Thanks."

Axel went in search of water, and Max pressed his eyes shut. *Pull it together, McRay*, he demanded internally. *You're in Michigan. Not Afghanistan. Now, tighten up.*

He concentrated on his breaths and brought images of Allie and Max Jr. into mind. This was his job, and he was good at it. Once he finished here, he could shower up and be with his family again, something he hadn't gotten to do twice in a row for far too long.

"Hey." Axel returned with a bottle of water and handed it to Max. "Anything else you need?"

"No." Adrenaline coursed through Max's veins as he sipped the cool liquid and scanned the scene around them once more.

This wasn't the desert. His leg was already gone. That mission was over. This one was still ahead.

"You're going to have one hell of a story for Allie tonight," Axel said, taking the nearly empty bottle when Max passed it back.

He forced a tight smile. A bead of sweat rolled over his temple. "No doubt."

Max had so much he needed to make right with Allie. He hadn't lived up to his vows or been what she deserved.

He knew that now. He'd known then, too, but he'd been too proud and stubborn to acknowledge it. The minute he'd pledged his allegiance to Allie, her needs should have come first. Above his, and before the TCD. She'd only wanted him to let her in. To include her in his decisions and travel plans. She'd wanted him to talk to her about his work, but he'd been so busy trying to keep his job and home life separate that he'd ended up being forced to choose between them. When he hadn't, she'd made the decision for him.

Max stared at the building. A possible bomb inside, waiting to explode.

And all he could think about was Allie.

A sharp whistle broke his reverie, and Sergeant Sims came into view. The local bomb-squad leader circled a finger in the air. Time to roll out.

Chapter Eleven

Sweat beaded on Max's forehead and temples as he moved onto the property, followed by two members of the Grand Rapids bomb squad in EOD suits. Mounting anxiety and the uncomfortably heavy gear worked in tandem to slow his every step. He pulled in long, steady breaths, moving through the mental techniques he'd once relied upon to get through each day. Deep inhalations through the nose, slow releases through the mouth. *Concentrate on one thing at a time*, he reminded himself. *Don't become waylaid by the big picture.*

He batted his eyes against a stinging drop of sweat, fallen from his forehead. The helmet that was part of his gear made it impractical to clear the drop properly, but Max would get by.

The crowd fell deadly silent as they watched the trio make their way up the walkway. An earlier sweep of the exterior perimeter had revealed nothing more than mounding snow and debris from local litterbugs along the building's edge.

Now it was time to move inside. He waved two

gloved fingers toward the open door. With the eyes of an entire county or more on them, thanks to the abundance of news crews, cell-phone cameras and the internet, Max gave a nod, then led the men inside.

He could only hope the bomber hadn't taken notice of the hoopla yet. If he had, and he'd planted a remotely detonated device, he could end the small squad's life at will.

He and the others split up at the mailboxes. One of the men moved onto the second floor, assigned to search the zone above the superintendent's small office space and apartment. The other man descended a secondary staircase to the basement, searching the area below.

Max stopped at the door marked as 101 and Staff. Henry hadn't seen O'Lear since he'd witnessed him fighting with the superintendent, but according to Teske, O'Lear had returned early this morning, ignoring the office hours Teske said he kept but none of the other tenants seemed to know of.

O'Lear delivered the rent as Teske had demanded, which thrilled the super, but he'd had to leave O'Lear alone in the office for a few minutes. Since Teske hadn't been expecting him, he'd had to return to his adjoining apartment for his glasses and to quiet his small dog.

If there was a bomb hidden in the building, Max suspected he would find it here.

He maneuvered the small key into the lock, then twisted until he felt the tumbler roll. His breath caught and silent prayers went up as the resulting click echoed through his body. The lock had released. Max hadn't blown up. He took a quick, steadying moment, then turned the knob and slipped cautiously inside.

Foreboding churned in Max's gut as he surveyed the surroundings. A large clock on the far wall indicated the time was eleven thirty. If Max's guess on O'Lear's plan was right, Max had thirty minutes to discover and disarm a ticking bomb.

ALLIE CREPT OUT of Max Jr.'s nursery, rubbing the aching muscles in her neck and rolling her head from side to side. She'd stayed home from the mall today as promised, but had gotten very little work accomplished. Instead, she'd carried, rocked and bounced her toddler for nearly two hours while he fought his fatigue and struggled with incoming teeth.

Now that it was finally quiet, she could only hope he would rest and she could focus.

She pressed her hands against the small of her back as she headed to the kitchen, stretching the bunched muscles along her spine.

She flipped on the television, then filled a glass with water and took a seat on the couch to unwind. A news bulletin swept across the screen before her first sip, and she felt her already tense muscles go into lockdown. "Please don't be another bomb," she said, pumping the volume a little higher with her remote. "Do not let Max be in danger."

A familiar reporter appeared on-screen, an expression of undeniable concern on her face. "The apartment building at Hayes and Vine has been completely evacuated by an FBI group known as the Tactical Crime Division, or TCD."

Allie's heart rate spiked. She climbed off the couch and ghosted to the television, leaving her water on the coffee table behind her.

"Even family pets have been removed from this south-side tenement, while a team of explosives experts search for Grand Rapids' third bomb."

Allie shook her head at the images before her, willing them not to be true. Crowds lined the streets outside an old yellow-brick building in a neighborhood she recognized near downtown. The door to the building gaped open.

"Sources say the FBI's TCD mobilized yesterday, deployed from the Traverse City headquarters, to investigate the two fatal bombings in Grand Rapids earlier this week. Less than twenty-four hours later, they've identified this man, Fritz O'Lear, as their prime suspect. O'Lear is believed to have had a personal connection to at least one fatally injured victim in each bombing, and records show him as a resident of the building being searched right now."

Allie's gaze fixed on the worried faces of Max's colleagues, and her heart nearly seized. Max's team was unflappable. If they were worried, she was terrified.

Allie jerked the cell phone from her back pocket and dialed her parents' number while she searched for her coat, purse and keys. "Mom?" she asked, the moment the call connected.

"I see it, baby," her mom said. "Your dad and I were just watching while we made lunch."

"I have to go," Allie said, a lump rising in her throat. "I need to be there. He's in there."

A soft knock sounded on her front door, and Allie raced to pull it open.

Her mom smiled, phone in one hand, emotion in her pale blue eyes. "Go. I'll stay with Max Jr. Your dad will bring lunch to me when it's ready."

Allie threw her arms around her mother, jammed her feet into boots, then made a run for her car, threading her arms into her coat sleeves as she hurried out.

Snow fell at an alarming rate as she barreled along city streets, racing toward the area where the news team had broadcasted. The roads were clear of ice and snow, but traffic was thick so close to lunchtime.

Allie worked to swallow and clear her head, but her heart ached with the idea she could be too late. She could lose Max, *really* lose him. And it hit her, for the first time, that she hadn't truly accepted their divorce as the end. She'd hoped that one day he'd get his head on straight and come back to her. His job was important, but so was she, so was their son, and though Max didn't seem to believe it, so was he. He could save the world and still have a family; he wasn't some tragic superhero out of a comic book.

Allie took every shortcut she could think of, scanning the radio for coverage of the situation. Instead of new information, she only received the same update on repeat. The FBI had named a bombing suspect, and they were sweeping a building right now.

Her stomach rolled as haunting images from the news returned to her. The concern on the reporter's brow. The fear in Max's teammates' eyes.

"I can't lose him," she muttered, taking another quick turn into an alleyway and darting down the pitted, unmaintained street.

When she reached the wooden barricades and shivering crowds, she parked along the curb and began to jog. "Axel!" She waved an arm overhead and yelled for her old friend as she drew near. "Axel!"

He turned, scanning the area until their eyes met. Then he began to move in her direction.

He swept the crime-scene tape high, waving off the approaching officer as Allie ducked beneath.

"Is he okay?" she asked. "What's happening?"

Axel set his hand against her back and ushered her into the little circle of TCD members at the end of the building's walkway.

The women pulled her into a series of hugs. The comfort and ease with which they accepted her back into the fold stung her eyes and nose, and threatened to tip her over the emotional edge. She'd worried they might hate her for leaving Max, but that didn't seem to be true.

"He's doing okay," Carly assured her, keeping

Allie against her side with one arm. "If anything had gone wrong, he would've contacted us."

Allie nodded. "Okay." She stared at the building, hoping Carly's words were true and willing her ex-husband to appear.

Axel shifted, turning back to the building. Selena and Aria stood with him, each statue-still. Their jaws were tight. Their backs rigid.

Allie pulled back from Carly, intuition lighting. "There's more," she accused. "There's something else. What don't I know?"

Carly didn't answer.

The others glanced her way, then went back to staring.

"Tell me," Allie demanded. "Please!" She covered her mouth, instantly horrified by the outburst.

Carly rubbed her palm up and down Allie's sleeve before stepping away to face her. "We think the bomber might've planned to detonate the device when his superintendent returned from lunch. At noon."

"Noon?" Allie raised her watch, then said a desperate prayer. It was already ten minutes till.

THE OFFICE SPACE was small and cramped. Max left the door open as he stepped inside. A battered metal desk stood on his immediate left, a rug in the center, and two plastic chairs with metal legs pressed against the opposite wall. Tall beige filing cabinets formed a row between an interior door to Teske's apartment and piles of ancient dust-covered boxes.

An evacuation map of the building hung above the cabinets, mostly blocked by a massive pair of faux ferns in cracked plastic pots. A century's worth of cigarette smoke had permeated everything. The air, the walls, the rugs.

Max examined the space, imagining O'Lear coming in to deliver the rent early this morning. He extended the retractable arm on his small tactical mirror and positioned it beneath the desk. No bomb. He opened the file cabinet drawers one by one. Then checked the desk drawers, as well.

He turned in a small circle, searching, thinking. Evaluating each object.

He had eight minutes to find and disarm a bomb or die.

Instinct pulled him to the stacks of ancient boxes. The thick layer of dust on one had been disturbed, as if the box on top of it had been moved.

Max unstacked the pile quickly, removing each lid as he went, then peeking inside for good measure. When he reached the box he'd been aiming for, his gut clenched in warning.

He lifted the cardboard top gently and froze at the sight of a pressure cooker.

The cheap digital watch attached to the lid had less than four minutes before it reached zero. When that happened, Max knew, the Tannerite, undoubtedly packed into the pot, along with every manner of metal projectile, would ignite.

The airtight container would stop the blast for a fraction of a second, creating unfathomable pressure, before exploding and blowing away everything in its path. The resulting fireball would be twenty feet across, blasting thousands of nuts and bolts, nails and BBs, along with bits of the destroyed pot, through the air, like shrapnel. Through everything in sight. And for more than a hundred yards. The red-hot, impossibly sharp bits would move at up to two thousand feet per second, faster than the speed of sound, and anyone in their range would be injured before they even heard the explosion. The shock wave would be felt up to a quarter mile away.

Footfalls on the stairs echoed through the otherwise silent building, and Max backed up until he could be seen through the door. He held one hand out before him like a crossing guard stopping traffic. The pair of local bomb-squad men froze. "I found it," Max said. "There's less than three minutes on the timer." He steeled himself, then forced every bit of authority he could muster into his words. "Go. I've got this." And if he didn't, there was no reason to lose three lives instead of one.

They hesitated, looking from the door, to one another, then back to Max.

"That's an order!" he shouted, imitating the drill sergeant he'd loathed as a new soldier, then admired as a seasoned veteran. "Now!"

The men shuffled quickly away.

Max turned back to the bomb, now at under two minutes, said a silent prayer and went to work.

The watch needed to come off first. He couldn't allow the alarm to activate while still attached to the cooker. Or the Tannerite. He stripped off the bulky safety gloves, his trained and nimble fingers suddenly shaking and unsure. With only one minute and four seconds left on the clock, he gripped the watch with sweat-slicked hands, counted mentally to three, then pulled. The watch separated cleanly from the pot, instantly stopping the timer.

ALLIE WRUNG HER frozen hands and paced. It was nearly noon, and every second felt like an eternity to her panicked, aching heart. The apartment building could go up in smoke at any minute, taking Max's life with it, and she didn't think she could live through that.

She pressed a gloved hand to her mouth to stave off the nausea, and batted away tears. She had to pull herself together. No matter what happened today or any day, Max Jr. needed her, and she needed to get tough for him.

A man in a dark suit broke away from the group of uniformed officers and headed for Axel.

Allie stopped pacing to watch.

The man's grim expression sent a bead of sweat over her brow despite the ferocious cold. "Special Agent Morrow." He handed Axel his phone. "I think you should see this."

Axel accepted the device, looked it over and paled.

"What is that?" Allie asked, unable to hold her tongue. "What's going on?" Her every instinct said whatever was happening had to do with Max, and it wasn't good.

Axel returned the man's phone, then shot Allie a remorseful look.

She could see the message in his eyes, practically hear the words running through his mind, but he was too polite to say them aloud. The specifics of the operation were classified, and she was an outsider. Never a member of the TCD, and no longer Max's wife.

The truth hit like a punch to her heart.

"Look!" Carly raised a pointed finger to the building as a figure appeared in the doorway.

Allie jumped forward, then slowed as two men in protective gear rushed down the walkway toward the sidewalk. Neither man was Max.

Tears blurred her vision and spilled across her cheeks. "Where is he?" she cried. "Where!"

Carly grabbed Allie's waist and held her tight as the men arrived.

"He found the bomb," the first man reported, struggling to remove his helmet and gloves. "There was less than three minutes. He sent us out."

Allie checked her watch, fear ratcheting in her heart.

It was noon.

"Stand back," a uniformed officer hollered through a bullhorn. "Move back now."

People scattered, rushing away from the yellow tape.

Axel cursed and moved forward.

Carly caught him by his arm.

Allie wanted to scream. She wanted to collapse. Why wasn't Max coming out? Why wasn't anyone going after him? What was happening?

"There he is!" Carly called. "Max!"

Allie's gaze snapped up, seeking the building and finding Max.

He strode confidently forward, the EOD helmet tucked securely under one arm, his gaze locked on hers.

She pushed her way through the group in a burst of joy, relief and awe.

He dropped his helmet and opened his arms as she launched herself at him.

Allie collided with his chest, nearly leaping into his arms, and he responded by holding her close.

He pressed his lips against her head and whispered, "I'm okay. It's okay."

She fought tears as the team filed in around them, along with at least a dozen local officials she'd never seen before and would never recognize in the future. All that mattered in that moment was that Max was all right, and they still had time to figure things out.

He held on to her as he debriefed the group on what had happened inside the building. Then she watched as Axel offered Max his cell phone.

"Local PD received this text message about four minutes ago," Axel explained.

Max accepted the device, and they looked at the screen together.

Three down, one to go. You won't be so lucky next time.

Kaboom.

"WHAT?" ALLIE LOOKED from Max to Axel, then back. "What does it mean?"

Max tightened his arm around her, pressing his fingers against her waist. "It means he isn't finished."

Chapter Twelve

Adrenaline coursed through Max's veins and lightened his head as he passed the cell phone back to Axel. Coming down from a moment like he'd just experienced inside always left him feeling slightly disoriented. He pulled Allie close once more, immeasurably thankful for her unexpected presence.

She fell easily against him, fear, relief and something deeper pooling in her eyes. She pressed her cheek to his chest, and his breaths began to settle. His heart rate started to slow. Small as she was, and fragile as she felt in his arms, Allie had always been his anchor. And the intense emotional connection flowing between them now was a drug he couldn't get enough of.

He spoke briefly with the bomb-squad captain, relaying the pressure cooker's location and pertinent details. The local team would take over from here, documenting the scene and arranging for removal and disassembly of the device. A bomb often told its maker's secrets, and Max could only hope that this one would give a hint to O'Lear's location, as well.

Max's teammates retreated, gathering near their SUVs while Max briefed the fire marshal and other officials with his findings and assessment. When he finished, his team gave him the space to say good-bye to Allie. He wanted to linger but had to hurry. He needed to get back to work before O'Lear retaliated. Max had ruined the bomber's planned attack, essentially stealing O'Lear's thunder, possibly humiliating him and making him feel exactly the same way he had when he concocted the deadly plan in the first place.

"I should go," Allie said, accurately interpreting the moment and stepping slowly away. She'd never been to a scene like this with Max before, and while her surprise presence had been momentarily comforting, he realized with a slap that it was time she got as far away from him as possible.

"Okay. Be safe," he said, glancing toward his team. "I'd better get back to work."

"Right," she said, sounding suddenly unsure. "Of course." She took a fumbling step back, hurt gathering in her eyes. "Maybe call if you won't be able to make it for dinner?"

"Of course." He nodded, scanning the crowd for signs of O'Lear and hoping that if the bomber stumbled on-site at this moment, he wouldn't understand how much Allie meant to him.

He hurried to his team with long, hungry strides, refusing to let himself look back.

Aria cringed as he approached. Selena shook her head. Axel's attention was somewhere else completely, his gaze trailing something in the distance. Max knew without asking that Axel was watching Allie. He'd keep tabs on her as long as possible, stepping in for Max when he couldn't keep her safe.

When Max turned to check his assumption, there was only a heavy crowd and line of reporters.

Allie was already gone.

The realization that his connection to her had suddenly become her biggest danger was enough to buckle his knees. How could he protect her if he couldn't get near her? And how could he make her understand his behavior today was meant to keep her safe when she'd surely see the exchange as a repeat of so many others during their married life? Of him dismissing her because work called. He could send a quick text, but what would he say? Would she see it as an excuse?

"Max?" Axel asked, prompting a response to a question Max hadn't heard.

"Yeah." Max forced himself back to the crisis at hand. "Let me pack up this suit, and I'll be ready to go."

He sloughed off his cumbersome EOD suit and freed the cell phone from his pocket to send Allie a text.

Sorry I had to run. I will be there tonight. Nothing can keep me away.

But he would be staying at the hotel moving forward. Allie's safety, and the safety of Max Jr., was top priority in Max's world. Everything else could get in line.

CARLY'S HEART WENT out to Allie as she watched her hurry away, then to Max as he rubbed the back of his neck, visibly struggling to get his head in the game. Carly understood the confliction. She'd been the agent taking lead on a case at Christmas, and she'd fallen in love in the process. Those two worlds, love and job, should never collide because it was terrifying. She'd worried for Noah as the case grew trickier, afraid something awful could happen to him because of his involvement and proximity to her. Now the tides had turned, and Noah was the one constantly worried about her every time she was called out on a case. Relationships were tricky for everyone, but for a TCD agent in love with a civilian, relationships were downright complicated.

Max lifted his eyes to hers, catching her staring.

She smiled, and he nodded, a silent exchange that told her she wasn't off base with her deductions. He'd just single-handedly located and disarmed a bomb, at the last second, then found his ex-wife waiting for him on the sidewalk. He'd likely also realized that the bomber was watching. Which had potentially put a target on her back.

"Let's take this meeting inside, shall we?" Carly asked, speaking up while Max pulled himself together.

She tipped her head toward the row of reporters and cameras, all angling for a look at them and the bomb-squad robot being deployed. The robot was fascinating. She could admit that it was fascinating, and not something most people saw every day. The robot would collect the device and seal it inside a container to take to the lab for deconstruction. But unlike the crowd, the TCD had work to do.

The team broke up, climbing into their SUVs for a rendezvous at their temporary headquarters. They'd take notes and text updates to Rihanna from the meeting, and she would do the same in return, sending details from the scene.

Carly raised her hand to Rihanna as the SUVs pulled away from the curb. Rihanna had hit the ground running as liaison the moment she'd arrived on-site, heading into the mix of reporters and before a buzzing crowd of local residents, determined to soothe nerves and deliver accurate information before rumors led to panic.

Traffic was light through town as Carly followed the SUVs in front of her. Axel driving Max, and Aria driving Selena, who was so turned around without Blanca in tow that she'd left the hotel this morning with dog treats in her pockets. The women had laughed about it at the time, but Carly could see Selena was as eager to get home as any of them.

The Grand Rapids Police Department was a flurry of activity when Carly and the team arrived. Officers rushed in and out of the main entrance and through the secured inner lobby. Phones rang off the hook at every desk, and the white noise of walkie-talkies filled the air.

"It's like someone kicked a hornet's nest in here," Carly said, making her way down the narrow hall to the conference room.

Aria smiled, looking a bit nostalgic for her days in blue. She'd been a Traverse City cop while earning her criminal justice degree. Neither was an easy feat. Succeeding at both at once was some other-level stuff. And Aria had definitely succeeded. The rookie had taken down a drug kingpin before Director Suzuki picked her up for the TCD team. "Once this bomb hit the news, these guys were probably instantly underwater," Aria said. "Anonymous tippers, witnesses hoping to help break the case, nuts wanting attention, people afraid their building will be next."

Carly smiled. Aria was right. Chaos always came quickly after something this big went public. The Grand Rapids PD would have their hands full calming a fearful population and stopping criminals determined to take advantage of the department's increase in calls and distractions.

Rihanna would do what she could, but ultimately the local media would make the difference in how things went from here. Unfortunately, sensationalism sold papers and gained viewers, so things typically got worse before the case was closed.

All the more reason to wrap this up ASAP. Panicky people were a danger all their own.

The team circled the conference-room table and took their seats. Axel powered up the projector and connected his laptop.

Opaline's face appeared on the screen. "Hello," she said instantly, glancing up while typing wildly on her keyboard. "Thank you for keeping me in the loop. I've got all your local news stations on my other monitors. And Rihanna is updating, as well. How are you all doing?"

The team gave a sober round of "Okays," "All rights" and "Fines."

Opaline's bright smile faltered. "Hmm." She leaned closer to the camera, stilling the room along with her. "Max," she said softly. "Can we just…?" She eased back, smile growing, and lifted her hands into view for a slow clap.

Carly smiled as Max shook his head and waved her off. Then she joined Opaline in the steady, appreciative rhythm. As did the rest of their team.

"Okay," Max said. He pushed up to stand, and the applause climbed to a crescendo before eventually coming to a stop. "Thank you," he continued. "Without all of your help, the fast action of this team and the local bomb squad, things could have gone a lot worse today." He blew out a shaky breath. "We were fortunate to get the result we did. Timing is everything right now, so we need to get back down to business or we could be a lot less lucky very soon."

Carly felt a tug of emotion in her chest as she took in his tone, expression and words. Max had done the real work today, putting the safety of others above himself. He'd overcome fear and likely some raging PTSD in the name of duty. Everyone on the team had been through tough things, but losing an appendage to a bomb, then making a career out of disarming the devices, was something completely beyond her ability to reason. She'd often thought that decision either spoke of true insanity or utter heroism. And she'd known Max long enough to say it wasn't the former. Yet he stood there, dividing the success of what he'd done among his teammates and others on scene.

Max smiled, and his dark brown eyes flickered with pride. He pressed his palms to the table and swung his attention to Opaline's bright expression on the screen. "Selena and Aria were smart to point out the pattern on these bombs. One bomb every other day with a rest day in between. It was only a hunch when she commented on it, but this bomb was set to detonate at noon. Three incidents make a pattern. Chances are O'Lear will wait another day, regroup and adjust his plan. Then we'll see the fourth attempt in forty to forty-eight hours, but there's also the chance he'll push his next move up to stay on schedule. We can't take any chances, especially after he sent that text message. We've ticked him off, and that's not good. So let's figure out who his next target will be and beat him to the location. Better yet, maybe even locate him before he makes his move."

"What do we know so far?" Carly asked, redirecting attention so Max could breathe.

He took his seat and waited for someone else to answer.

"We know he's watching," Selena said. "He sent the text. So he knows we're here."

"And working against him," Aria added. "We know he's not worried about collateral damage, and that he has at least one more hit on his list, based on his text. If he doesn't take another crack at the superintendent later."

Selena tapped her pointer finger against the desk, thinking. "What do we know about the number that text was sent from?" She turned to her sister, Opaline, on the screen.

The eyes of the TCD turned with her.

Opaline nodded. "I'm working on that. I've been able to confirm the number belongs to a burner phone, which is turned off. So I can't trace where the device is at the moment. But every phone has a serial number, and I'm running through a database of those numbers now, trying to get the serial number matching the phone number and phone used for that text. With that, I can determine which store the phone was shipped to and purchased from. Then I can request register receipts for a time stamp of the purchase, and look at corresponding surveillance videos to see if I can track his path visually when he leaves the store. Maybe get a look at what he's driving or anyone he speaks with."

Carly grinned. "Remind me to never try to hide from you."

Opaline chewed her lip. "You might give me a run for my money, but I'm going to find this guy soon. I've widened the scope of my search, and his photo is all over the news. Someone out there knows this guy, so if the PD phone lines are blowing up, that means folks are already trying to help out."

Axel shifted forward, resting his forearms on the table. "I'm hoping to have a warrant to get inside O'Lear's apartment this afternoon. We've got enough direct links from the bombs to this guy to make the request and get a quick signature from the judge. Chief Drees will keep me posted. The minute it comes in, I want a team over there."

"We can go," Carly offered, motioning to Aria and Selena on either side of her.

Axel cast a look in Max's direction, waiting for his feedback. Axel was the supervisory agent, but Max had taken lead on this case, and he'd saved a lot of lives today. If he said he wanted to be there, he would. Carly hoped he'd take some time to breathe first.

Max nodded. "Yeah. Sounds good. Keep me looped in."

Carly smiled. "Absolutely."

"All right." Axel turned his eyes back to the screen, where Opaline frowned furiously at something out of view. "Can you put together a list of possible targets from the information you have now?"

"Soon," she said, typing wildly on her keyboard, expression deadly serious. "I'll be in touch again the minute I have anything to share."

And with that, she was gone.

Chapter Thirteen

Opaline ordered her favorite Tex-Mex takeout on the way home and changed immediately into her pajamas once the food arrived. Her cats, Snape and Dobby, met her at the door, meowing and attempting to lead her to their food bowls.

She gave them pats, filled their bowls and scratched behind their ears, thankful for the safety and comfort of her apartment, a space where she could freak out, break down and take off her smile as needed. She'd forced the cheer and positivity today until she thought she'd lose it on-screen. She'd basically hung up on the group at the end of their last video conference. The smile was for them. They were in the thick of things, risking their lives, and the least she could do was to be a constant and reliable source of positivity.

Except she was fresh out of happy, and moving fast into rage and despair. If she didn't get her team some information they could actually work with soon, there would be another bombing, and more people would die.

Her chest tightened at the thought. Tonight was a work night. *A fight night.*

And Fritz O'Lear was her weaselly, no-good opponent.

She wore her favorite maroon-and-gold-striped cotton sleep pants and oversize T-shirt proclaiming Life's a Struggle When You're a Muggle. Though tonight she needed to be a wizard, at the keyboard at least. She whipped her hair into a messy bun, donned her fuzzy black socks, then carried her take-out to her workspace.

Dobby and Snape followed, having lost interest in the kibble once she'd opened the disposable container to steal a loaded nacho and inhale the cheesy, salty, spicy scents of her favorite chicken enchiladas. "You each get one bite," she said, pinching off a shred of chicken and offering the kitties a tiny little morsel. "I have to work. You have to go be adorable somewhere else until I take a break. No distractions. And you can't have any more of my dinner, so don't get any ideas." The cats stared, and Opaline caved. "Okay. One more bite, but that's it." She gave them each another taste before digging into her work.

"All right, O'Lear. It's time to stop this nonsense and show yourself." She forked a bite of enchilada, sipped the steamy coffee and got busy.

Opaline had been up against a lot of criminals in the past, but none with less of a digital footprint than this guy. Some of the younger nuts she'd chased through cyberspace had even bragged about their crimes. Gang members were the worst, or maybe the dumbest. Definitely the most prideful, posting images of themselves with rolls of cash, guns, drugs and everything else to their social-media accounts. They boasted. Called out enemies by name, and their latest hookups, too, often adding location tags. Those criminals were so easy to locate that they practically invited her to hang out. Fritz O'Lear, on the other hand, was giving her fits.

She crossed her legs on the office chair, then powered up her laptop. Four independent screens flickered to life on her desk. She selected her favorite, work-all-night playlist, popped her phone onto the speaker dock, then snagged another nacho.

"Who are you, Fritz O'Lear?" she asked for what felt like the thousandth time in a few days. Serial bombers and psychotic killers didn't live in a vacuum. Someone knew this guy. And someone had gotten a bad vibe from him along the line. She needed to find one of those people. O'Lear or the person who knew where to find him. She wasn't picky.

Fritz O'Lear was just old enough to have missed spending his youth online, and apparently he'd never picked up the lifestyle. If he had an email address for personal use, it was registered under an alias, because she couldn't find it. He didn't have a LinkedIn profile, nor a Twitter account. His Facebook page hadn't been updated in years, and even then he'd barely bothered to use it. He claimed to like country music and a handful of old sitcoms in his barely completed profile. Grand Rapids was listed as his hometown, and the local high school as his alma mater. He only had a handful of friends and no family listed.

Not exactly a treasure trove of information.

Opaline opened each of his friends' profiles in new windows and scrutinized their lives, looking at how and where they'd intersected with O'Lear through the years. She scanned his personal photos and images where others had tagged him. Noted places in town where he'd spent time, then followed each of his friends around the world wide web. Jumping platform to platform, attempting to understand O'Lear by getting to know his friends. The more she understood who he was, the easier it would be to find him.

One pal stood out, and his name was Mark Waters. According to a photo Mark had tagged him in, the two were "lifelong friends." Unfortunately, that lead, like all the others, came to a dead end, literally, when Mark's obituary surfaced. He'd been in an accident ten months ago. But Opaline wasn't letting go of a lead that easily. Instead, she used the online memorial page to track down Mark's parents, who conveniently still lived in town. A lifelong friend of their son's might be someone his family remembered, maybe even someone they'd known personally.

She thought of messaging some of Fritz's other social-media friends, using an alias, to ask if they knew where Fritz was because she had to get in touch with him about some money he'd inherited.

But that could accidentally alert him to her search, so she held off. She'd use that tactic if necessary, but first she'd try tracking down this Mark fellow's family.

Snape climbed onto Opaline's lap after midnight, purring and sniffing the nearly empty take-out containers. She stroked his fur, thankful for the kitty comfort, but wholly dissatisfied with her progress on the case. She needed a smoking gun. But all she'd managed to find was smoke. Nothing tangible. Nothing concrete.

"What do you think, Snape?" she asked, a yawn opening her mouth wide. "We need more than the names of an old friend's family members to offer the team tomorrow. We need the name and location of someone who's actually talked to this guy in the past year. Preferably on a personal level, not the employees at Ramsey Realty."

Snape stretched on her lap and bumped his head against her chin, nuzzling and purring more loudly. He kneaded his paws against her middle, then curled into a fluffy black ball on her lap.

OPALINE'S HEAD FELL suddenly forward at two thirty in the morning. She let out a yelp, and Snape screeched away. "Sorry," she whispered, pushing onto her feet for a stretch.

She went to the kitchen and tucked her food containers into the fridge. Then she bumbled into the bathroom to splash cold water on her face. From there, she put on a pot of coffee.

Images of Max's expression as he'd walked out of that building, half stunned, half horrified, burned in her mind. Opaline had waited with the masses, holding her breath and sending up silent prayers that he would return at all. She tried to imagine what kind of person it took to go into a building and look for a bomb. Then to find a device counting down, with only three minutes left before detonation, and not turn away and run. How did anyone do that? Especially someone who'd nearly died doing the exact same thing once before.

A brewing tear-storm stung her eyes and nose. Mental and emotional fatigue weighted her limbs. Her throat clogged, and a sudden sob broke in her chest.

Lives were at stake. Lots of lives. Including the lives of her teammates. And her sister.

Tears spilled, hot and fast, over her cheeks.

Fritz O'Lear had been prepared to murder forty people today. He had to be stopped. The TCD was ready. But they couldn't stop him if they couldn't find him, and that was on her.

And she was failing.

She thought again of the images she'd seen on television. All those pets and people O'Lear had been ready to blow up so he could feel powerful for one second. So he could punish someone who'd made him feel weak. And she thought of the funerals that were coming tomorrow and the next day, as his recent victims were laid to rest. The families they left behind, forever changed because O'Lear had been rejected, because he'd been teased.

Opaline scrubbed heavy hands across her face and against her eyes as determination overtook despair. She wiped tears and shook away the feelings of failure and fatigue. She had the rest of her life to question her skills and beat herself up, right after she got back in her chair and helped her team.

She poured a bowl-sized mug of black coffee and marched back to her desk. She couldn't physically defend her teammates on the front line, but she could have their backs on her turf. Online. She could and would get them the information they needed to stay safe and protect others. And she wouldn't stop trying until she succeeded.

She didn't lower her head again until the sun began to rise.

shut that bomb down, all I could think of was you and Max Jr. I was terrified I'd never see you again, and I hadn't made things right between us. Then I walked outside, you were there, and I thought, *This is my chance. I can do the right thing.*"

She crossed her arms and chewed her lip.

He recognized the defensive posture and pressed on before she shut him down. "I pulled away from you today because I realized that if the bomber sent that text, then he knew I was there, and that I'd stopped his attack. Whether he was in the crowd, or watching from another location, I couldn't be sure, but if he had eyes on the scene and saw you with me…" Max trailed off, unable to voice the unthinkable truth.

Allie's expression softened, and her arms fell loose at her sides. "He might've seen you holding me."

"I didn't want him to see you anywhere near me." Max groaned. He leaned a hip against the counter and scrubbed a heavy hand over his face, the scruff of his beard grinding against his palm. "The realization that my feelings for you could put you in danger—" he swallowed hard, forcing the words through a tightening jaw "—was a hell of a lot scarier than any bomb."

A fresh blush washed over Allie's cheeks, and she turned away to slice the bread. "You were protecting me," she said shyly. "I'm not sure how I misinterpreted that. I guess it's what you do."

Max moved into the space behind her and set a

tentative hand on her lower back. "I also have a bad habit of hurting you, and I wish I could take that pain back. I gave you the impression my work was more important than my family, and it's just not true."

Allie stilled her knife against the bread. Her body tensed.

"Dada!" Max Jr. called. He smacked his highchair tray and squealed. "Dada! Dada!" He released a long round of raspberries with his tongue, and Allie laughed.

Max moved away from Allie. "I've got this." He opened the cupboard and collected one of Max Jr.'s plastic plates, then a baby spoon and fork from the rack. "I think he's trying to tell us how delicious this meal smells, and how much he'd like some. Right now."

Allie smoothly moved a few baby carrots and tiny potatoes onto the little plate beside some bits of roast.

Max sliced the food for their son, then followed Allie to the table. She set the pan with her roast and vegetables on a wooden trivet, then took a seat beside Max Jr.'s high chair.

"We still make a good team," Max said, enjoying the familiar ease of working at her side.

"Teamwork was never one of our problems," she said, serving roast and potatoes to Max, then portioning some for herself. "You and I were always good together."

Something in her tone sent heat through Max's

core, and a surge of unbidden, deeply intimate memories of their early days together flooded into mind.

"Do you really think I could be in danger?" she asked.

The thought doused Max in ice.

Allie's gaze flickered to Max Jr., then back. "Could *we* be in danger?"

"I don't know," he admitted, tension returning to his muscles, gripping his back, neck and shoulders painfully. "I can't be sure what the bomber saw today."

"Maybe you should go back to your hotel tonight," she said softly. "It's not that I don't want you to be here. I just don't want to take the risk. What if he follows you?"

Max turned his attention to the meal before him, hoping to hide his horror at the possibility. He'd been careful, but what if he'd missed something? "I understand why you'd say that, and it makes sense on the surface," he said.

Eventually he wiped his mouth on his napkin and refocused on the gorgeous blonde across from him.

"But," she guessed.

His lips twitched, and he fought a small smirk. She knew him so well. Unfortunately, he'd taken a risk by coming for dinner, even if the extremely overdue apology he owed Allie seemed paramount at the time. Now that he was there, it was too late to turn back. "I'm already here," he said. "I can't be sure O'Lear doesn't know that. Leaving you alone could be the opposite of helpful, if he knows this is where I came after work."

Her shoulders sagged before squaring once more. Her expression was unreadable.

"I won't let anything happen to you or Max Jr.," he vowed.

"I know." Allie pushed the food around her plate, clearly thinking, but not saying a word. Max could only imagine where her thoughts had gone. His job might've put her in danger. Exactly what he'd tried to avoid throughout their relationship.

"You were a real help, going to the station and working with the sketch artist," he said, changing the subject. "I don't think I thanked you properly for that. Knowing you saw him watch the Burger Mania blast goes a long way toward building our profile. Combined with the text he sent today, I can confidently say this guy likes to watch the explosions. He enjoys the destruction and seeing the chaos unfold. We think he takes a day between bombings to bask in the power rush."

Allie paled. Her chewing slowed, and she turned her eyes on their baby. "Do you think there's any chance he recognized me? From that night in the car? Then again at the scene today?"

The food turned to sawdust on Max's tongue as the remote possibility took hold. How could he stay another minute with Allie if being there could put a target on her? And how could he leave if Fritz O'Lear already had her in his sights?

How could Max know if either was true?

ALLIE CLEANED THE kitchen after dinner, watching and listening as Max played with and cared for their son. The moments were bittersweet and nostalgic, and she didn't want Max to go. She missed hearing his voice and laughter. She missed his comforting and protective presence. She missed his touch.

She scrubbed the table a little harder, attempting to distract herself from the growing sense of loss, knowing he had to leave again soon. She'd spent the months after her divorce the same way, trying to distract herself from the pain. She'd joined a gym, thrown herself into her work and concentrated on being the very best mother she could. But one look at Max, lying on his back on her living-room floor, with their son held above him like a tiny superhero, was ripping apart any progress she'd made.

She put on a kettle for tea and arranged a pair of mugs beside the stove. Max used to tease her for her preference for tea over coffee, but he'd learned to appreciate the drink. Like she'd learned to appreciate draft beer. He'd begun to go on morning runs with her. She'd started joining him in the weight room at his gym. She and Max had always been a perfect team of give-and-take. Teacher and student. Partners in every sense of the word. Until the TCD called, and his real team took him away for days, even weeks on end. Usually at the drop of a dime. Always to rescue or protect another family.

Until today, all those missions had been abstract. They'd felt false. Distant. Not worth letting him go at every turn. But being there today with the crowds and the team had changed that. She'd felt the suffo-cating tension and fear in the air, and she'd seen the faces of all those residents as they were moved to a safe location. The helpless pets loaded into crates. The elderly. The children. It had nearly torn her heart in two.

And knowing Max had saved all those people by putting their lives and safety ahead of his own had given Allie a brand-new perspective on absolutely everything. Including what she needed from Max, if he was willing to consider it.

She dried her hands on a towel and moved to the island that separated her kitchen and living room, greedy for a closer look at the two most amazing men in her life.

They were seated now, a book between them. Max Jr. yawned and rubbed his eyes.

"Aw. Hey, now," Max said, steadying their wob-bly son. "Looks like someone's getting tired." He set the book aside, then cuddled Max Jr. to his chest before rising gracefully to his feet.

Allie admired the long, lean muscles of Max's body, and the fluidity with which he moved. It was so easy to forget a prosthetic limb replaced his lower left leg and foot. He'd nearly died before they met. It was unbelievable how close she'd come to never meeting him. If everything that happened after that blast hadn't happened exactly as it did, Allie's life would have been completely different, as well. But she chose to believe that fate had saved him for her, because from the moment they'd met, Max had been her everything. He was the reason she believed in soul mates.

"I think I might've worn him out," Max said, cradling Max Jr. in his arms. "Do you mind if I do the routine tonight? Is it still a diaper, a song and a kiss?"

Her heart swelled. Max remembered that, too? She'd never thought he'd paid much attention to her bedtime routine with the baby. "Yeah," she said. "It hasn't changed." It was too bad so many other things had.

Max smiled. "Then I'll be back in a few minutes."

Allie tiptoed to the baby monitor and powered it on, listening as Max spoke softly to their son. He whispered a story as he changed his diaper. Then he began to sing.

Max Jr. cooed and gurgled, fighting sleep without crying, a definite improvement over the last few miserable nights of teething.

She drifted back to the kitchen and turned off the kettle, no longer interested in tea. Then she slipped into the bathroom to check her hair and face in the mirror. Her cheeks were flushed and her eyes were wild. Pretty much what she'd expected. She took a moment to settle her thoughts, then headed back into the hallway to wait for her ex-husband.

He'd told her he was leaving tonight, but she had something she needed to do before she let him go.

Max crept from the nursery several minutes later and pulled the door shut behind him. He narrowed his eyes when he saw her, though she doubted he hadn't known she was there. He'd always seemed to know where she was. How she was feeling. And what was on her mind. "Can we talk before I go?"

Allie stepped forward, wetting her lips and pushing away from the wall. "We don't have to talk," she said. "I know your time is limited, and I don't want to keep you, if you're sure that leaving is for the best."

Max stilled, his brows coming together in confusion. "What?"

"I understand how much you're needed on this case," she said, feeling the confession begin to flow. "I realize how selfish I was before. I couldn't see it then, but I do now. And I'm sorry."

Max moved closer, his eyes locked with hers. "I'm the one who owes you an apology. You and Max Jr. have always been my priority, but I didn't act like it."

Allie's attempts to keep herself from falling apart ended with his words. She closed the remaining gap between them and rose onto her toes to kiss him.

Max tensed, momentarily, as her lips grazed his, then quickly came to life under her touch. His arms curled around her back as she sank against him. His mouth met hers, press for press, and she moaned as he deepened the kiss.

Heat licked over her neck and chest, then pooled low in her core. She stepped back, fuzzy-headed and infinitely lighter, lips full from the urgency of their kiss.

Max looked equally dazed, a small smile on his slack, handsome face.

"Sorry. You said you wanted to talk?" she asked, trailing her fingertips down the hard planes of his chest. "I interrupted."

He rubbed a palm over his face, then pierced her with a pointed stare. "I wanted to tell you I was scared today," he said. "I had flashbacks, and the PTSD hit so hard I didn't think I could get past it. Somehow, I pushed through. Then I found that bomb, and I had clarity about what's important and how badly I screwed up. I knew what I'd done wrong. I understood why you left me. And I know I need to say so."

Allie let her hands fall away, shocked and utterly unnerved at the unexpected change of subject and sudden tension between them.

Max caught her hands and pressed them against his heart, covering her fingers with his. "I thought that keeping you separate from my job would keep you safe, but not letting you in was a mistake. You deserved answers to your questions, then and now. You asked me how I was feeling when I got here, and I skipped around it. The truth is that I was nervous to see you. I was terrified that I'd ruined things for good when I pulled away without explanation this afternoon. I was hopeful that I didn't, and I'm still finding my way through the residual panic of the bomb. The one I disarmed today, and the one that nearly killed me all those years ago. I never talk about my feelings, because I don't like to, and I don't talk about losing my leg because it's hard to manage the memories. I don't want you to think of me as weak. Because I can't protect you if I'm weak."

Allie started to respond, but Max took a deep breath, and she knew he hadn't finished.

"It's no excuse for pushing you away before," he said, looking more guilty and ashamed than anyone she'd ever seen, "but once I found out you were pregnant, I went from being overjoyed to being terrified. I let the PTSD take ahold of me, and I spent every day knowing that if something happened to you, I'd lose the both of you, and it was more than I could stand. So I pulled away, cowardly. I was angry with myself for not being stronger, for keeping you upset, for failing you. I became consumed by the negatives. I hid behind my job, and I lost sight of what was right here in front of me. I am deeply sorry." He pulled her close and swept the backs of his fingers across her cheek, tucking hair behind her ears and looking at her as if she was the only thing that had ever mattered. "I'm able to say all that now, because I took your advice after the divorce. It was too late to save us, but I talked to someone at the VA who helped me figure out my mess."

Allie's breath caught, and hope curled through her heart. All she'd ever wanted was to be a part of Max's life. *His whole life.* She wanted him to trust her with his feelings and talk to her like she was his best friend, because he had always been hers. She'd told him those things a thousand times, but she'd never thought he heard her. His unexpected confession meant more to her than anything else he could possibly have done. She turned her hands in his and squeezed. "It doesn't have to be too late."

She cupped his cheek, caressing the sweet stubble and rising back onto her toes. "You are all I've ever wanted. But I need all of you, not just the pieces you think are best. You have to trust me with everything. Like our marriage vows said, for better and for worse. I need more than a protector, Max. I need a partner. And so do you." She locked her stubborn gaze with his remorseful one. "Even fancy explosives experts and war heroes need someone to take care of them once in a while."

A slow smile spread over Max's handsome face. "Are you offering?"

Allie pressed her lips to his, then curled her fingertips in the material of his shirt. She stepped backward, tugging him toward her bedroom. "I am."

He followed easily, still smiling. "You think I'm fancy?"

Allie laughed as she closed her door behind them and pressed him against it. "I do. Now shut up and kiss me."

Chapter Fifteen

Max woke to the sounds and scents of breakfast. Running water, the gentle clang of pans and soft sizzle of bacon floated to his ears in the small one-story home. Allie's sweet voice rose above it all as she sang a silly song, presumably to their little boy. A smile broke across Max's face as he let the moment settle in.

He was glad Allie had agreed to let him stay last night. Honestly, he wasn't sure he could have brought himself to leave. If she'd insisted, he'd probably have slept in his car outside her front door. He wasn't completely sure how he could leave her today. Or ever again, but that was something he'd have to work out later. They'd have plenty to talk about, and some complicated things to figure out, once his case was closed and it was time for him to return to Traverse City. Like, did she mean it when she'd said there was still a chance for them? For more than a few nights?

Max swung himself out of bed and reached for his prosthesis. He arranged the heavy liner at the bottom of his residual limb, then rolled it slowly up his leg, careful not to leave any air against his skin inside the liner. He bent his knee to pull on the device, then rolled the sleeve up his thigh. He dressed slowly, taking time to wake up and enjoying the moment. The scent of Allie's cooking in the air, and the scent of her on his skin.

Max Jr.'s laugh trickled down the hall, pulling Max to the kitchen. The toddler shoved chubby fistfuls of dry cereal and strawberries into his mouth while Allie flipped bacon in a frying pan. She sang a song Max didn't recognize, full of animal names and rhymes. Then she turned to bow for their son.

Both men clapped.

"Hey!" Allie pointed her spatula at Max. "No creeping."

"I was admiring," he said. "Can you blame me?"

She grinned, cheeks pink and wearing his white V-neck T-shirt like a nightgown. "When the person you're admiring doesn't know she's being watched, it's called creeping," she said. "I should call the FBI about you." She turned back to a pan of scrambled eggs beside the bacon.

"Please do," he said. "I know a guy who'd love to get your call anytime." Max kissed his son's head, then poured a mug of coffee, taking his time before he reached his ex-wife. "I've missed this," he said, setting a hand on her back and leaning in to kiss her cheek. "I've missed you."

"Back at ya," she said, shooting him an impish look. "How'd you sleep?"

Max laughed. "Deeply. I haven't slept for six hours straight in months."

"Have you ever?" she asked. "I remember you sneaking out of bed most nights when we were married. Into your office to work."

Max sipped his coffee, remorseful for all the time he could've spent with her, but he'd willingly stayed away. He probably hadn't slept a full night since he'd joined the military. Definitely not since joining the TCD, but he could've spent those sleepless hours in her arms instead of buried in his work. "I'm not sure how you got away this morning without me noticing."

Allie turned the fire off under each pan, then offered Max a sad smile. "Maybe the fact you haven't slept in the better part of a decade had something to do with it."

"Maybe," he said, admiring her body as she ferried a plate of eggs to their son. Her legs were long and lean, visible nearly to her perfect backside in that shirt, and he ached to take her back to bed.

"Hungry?" she asked.

"Ravenous."

She blushed again, and he had to remind himself there was a toddler in the room.

Determined to behave himself, and enjoy another family breakfast before he had to go, he fixed two plates of eggs and bacon, then carried them to the table.

"Thanks," Allie said, taking a seat.

Max lowered onto the chair across from her, then

dug into his meal. It didn't take long before a sliver of guilt wiggled into his bliss. The rest of his team had likely lost sleep last night, chasing leads and trying to find the bomber. Max had essentially taken a vacation.

"You're frowning," Allie said. "What's wrong?"

He forced a smile and nearly told her it was nothing, then remembered that move had cost him everything once before. "I'm wondering how things went with the search of O'Lear's apartment, and if there were any more bomb threats or news since I fell asleep."

Allie considered him. "You haven't checked your phone?"

Max fished his phone from his pocket, shocked that it hadn't been the first thing he'd done when he woke.

"I can also say with complete certainty that if your team had needed you, they'd have shown up at my door and knocked it down if necessary."

He laughed at the imagery. She wasn't wrong about them coming for him, if they'd truly needed him.

"Don't feel bad for getting some sleep," she said. "You can't be at your best when you're running on empty. It's as if you did them all a favor. You'll be sharper from the rest."

Max scrolled through his missed texts and emails. Chief Drees had come through with a warrant to search O'Lear's apartment just before Max stopped back at the hotel to shower and change for dinner with Allie. The team had sent regular updates with photos and appeared to have carefully overturned every object in a show of extreme due diligence. A footlocker in the back of his closet held enough evidence to link O'Lear to both blasts and to the bomb in Teske's office. Packaging and receipts for four pressure cookers. Multiple Tannerite containers, and a mother lode of empty labeled containers meant for nails, bolts and BBs.

And a journal.

Max smiled. If the bomb-making materials alone could have possibly been argued in court as circumstantial, the detailed personal account of O'Lear's perceived wrongs, his plans for action and the step-by-step guide to building and detonating his bombs would put him away for life. All that was missing were the names of his targets. O'Lear had only used pronouns.

Simultaneous relief and anxiety flushed through Max as he processed the news. The TCD had everything they needed to put O'Lear away, but they still hadn't found him, and they didn't know when or where he'd attack again.

And to make matters worse, O'Lear had probably seen his apartment being searched, which meant he knew they had him. With nothing left to lose, someone as unhinged as the Grand Rapids bomber would become more dangerous than ever.

"Meeting at eight," he said, tucking the phone back into his pocket.

The team had been busy, but they'd gotten along just fine while he'd rested.

He went back to his meal, itching to hear more about O'Lear's apartment search straight from his colleagues' mouths. He'd also like to stop by and take a look for himself. If he hurried, he could get to the station early enough to spend some time with the emails he'd just flipped through and familiarize himself with all the information he'd missed last night, before the meeting began.

Allie wiped her pretty mouth with a napkin, her plate nearly empty. "I can see your mental wheels turning. You're eager to get out there and chase the bad guy."

"I am," he admitted, drawn back to the moment, to the good things in his life, and away from the darker pieces. "Can I see you again tonight?"

"Yes, please," Allie said, smiling sweetly across the small table.

It took more willpower than he thought he had, but Max removed himself from the table, showered and dressed for work. He kissed Allie and their baby goodbye at the door. The moment felt a lot like old times, except better. There was a new peace and understanding between him and Allie now, one he wished he'd been able to facilitate a year ago, before the divorce papers had arrived.

"Be safe, okay?" she said, a hint of fear in her warm hazel eyes. "And come back to me."

He wasn't sure if she'd simply meant for him to come back for the evening, or if there'd been a bigger request in the words. Either way, he'd absolutely return to her. And he'd stay, gratefully, for as long as she'd allow him. "I promise."

FRITZ O'LEAR HAD watched as nervous cops and anxious reporters gathered around his apartment building. As the infuriating bomb squad and some FBI goons stopped his third bomb.

He'd watched as the interfering lawmen passed his text message among themselves, trading cautious looks and scanning the crowd for signs of the sender.

He'd watched as they later returned to rummage through his things. To steal from him, and to try to stop him, which they couldn't.

Fritz saw everything. He'd even cased the ritzy hotel on the edge of town where the team was staying. He'd seen their matching SUVs there last night when he'd headed to a dingy motel outside the city limits, where he could pay with cash and no identification was required.

He hated everything about the feds' hotel. Too tall. Too showy. Too self-important. Just like all of them. He'd parked across the street, considering.

Should he add one more location to his list of targets? Wouldn't blowing up the team who'd come to stop him make the perfect finale to his show?

Hiding a bomb in a hotel would be easy. People came and went all the time. And no one paid any attention.

He'd slipped out of his car and walked the perimeter of the hotel, getting a feel for the job. He could take his time exploring the building's interior tomorrow, when the agents left for work. He couldn't be sure when they might return tonight. Likely on high alert, and all wound up from their little victory.

The agents probably assumed their win earlier in the day meant they were better than him, but they were wrong, and he'd make sure they knew. The FBI had interfered. Broken into his home. Taken his things. And it was time they were put in their places. Reminded who was in charge.

Then, in a perfect twist of fate, as Fritz had made his way back around the building, the big glass doors to the hotel's lobby parted, and the agent who'd stopped his bomb walked out. Alone. Fritz had hated him since the moment he'd seen him on television. With his flawless brown skin and that peculiar, cocky strut. This one was all superiority, muscles and attitude. Probably trained to disarm bombs in some high-tech federal facility. A man who'd never known real problems in his life but had made a career out of causing others, like Fritz, trouble. And that just wasn't okay.

Fritz had waited while the man climbed into an obnoxious government vehicle in the hotel parking lot, and then Fritz had made a run for his car. His old-model Toyota wasn't new or expensive like the SUV he followed through town, stopping at a bakery and another little shop, but it was too old for GPS tracking and still registered to the previous owner, a friend who'd died in a motorcycle accident. Which made Fritz untraceable. A ghost.

Chapter Sixteen

Max arrived at the station early, as planned. He greeted the officers he passed on his way to the conference room, already beginning to recognize many of the morning crew and a few of those finishing the night shift.

He carried his quickly cooling cup of drive-through coffee toward the TCD's temporary headquarters, then slowed as the door came into view. Light spilled unexpectedly through the small rectangular window, suggesting he wasn't the first to arrive, despite the time. Most of his team had been awake through the night, sending emails and correspondence as he'd slept. Those agents should have slept until the last minute and be arriving as the meeting began. At least, that had been the norm for the past seven years.

Max reached the door, still guessing who might be inside. Grand Rapids PD had been directed to stay out when a member of the TCD wasn't present, and the cleaning crew had the same orders. Maybe Rihanna, the only teammate he hadn't received any overnight messages from, had gotten a jump on her day. Or maybe one of the others simply couldn't sleep. Sometimes insomnia trumped fatigue when investigators got this close to catching a killer. Adrenaline-laced anticipation could be impossible to ignore.

He swung the door open and stepped inside, unable to make a guess. Regardless, he would have been wrong.

Director Suzuki sat at the front of the table, signing a stack of papers and saying her goodbyes to a vanishing face on the screen where Opaline would soon appear. "Good morning, Max," she said, barely looking up.

"Director." He went to the front of the room and set his coffee on the conference table across from her. "I didn't know you were coming into town. Is everything okay?" He could only hope she wasn't there to drop a massive figurative bomb in his lap. Something about Fritz O'Lear. A game changer that would set the team back to square one.

"Yes," she said. "All is well." She signed another paper, then set her pen aside. Poised and graceful as always, and not a hair out of place, she folded her hands in her lap. Her tailored navy suit was unwrinkled. Her legs crossed. "I'm here to meet with Chief Drees and the commissioner about the progress we've made so far. They're pleased with Rihanna's work, but you know I like to leave my mark whenever I can." Her smile was small, warm and mildly defensive.

Max suspected she was there to make sure her team was being treated well and had everything they needed, no holdups, red tape or resistance of any kind.

"How are you, Max?"

"Good. Thanks."

"You're early. The morning meeting won't begin for another forty minutes," she said, evaluating gaze roaming over his face. "Were you able to sleep?"

"I did," he said, struck once more with guilt for that truth. "I thought I'd come in a little early and review the information we have so far. Maybe ferret out a potential next move or find a new lead. Something I could offer at the meeting."

Alana watched him, assessing, he assumed. She'd no doubt seen the footage of him at the bomb site like everyone else in Michigan, via local news and the internet. And Max was sure she'd spoken with Axel, the supervisory agent, about Max's state of mind after the fact.

It wasn't uncommon for Alana to meet with the local officials in a case like this one, but she always did that by phone or video conference. "You don't normally visit field sites. Is there anything of particular concern here?"

Her lips tipped up at the sides. "Yes. You."

"Me?" He felt his brows furrow.

"This is a big case for you," she said.

Max's muscles tightened. He didn't like where this was going. "Yes, ma'am."

"We've chased bombers before," Alana said. "But

this case is different. We aren't here to assist in a manhunt after a major attack. This is the TCD's first active bomber case. And you haven't had to face off with an explosive device like you did yesterday since before we met."

Max dipped his chin, once, in agreement. Tension rolled down his spine, and the phantom pain he sometimes felt, where his leg no longer existed, plucked at him, begging him to reach for it. But he refused. Lacing his fingers on the table where his hands were folded instead.

"You did a miraculous thing," she said. "Brave. Professional. Effective." She paused until his eyes met hers. "Heroic."

"Necessary," he countered.

Her smile faded and her sharp brown eyes narrowed. "You did a good job out there, Max. I came here to say so, in case you missed the memo."

He frowned. "You came to Grand Rapids to check up on me?" Max wasn't sure if that was heartwarming or a sign she thought he needed babysitting.

"Impressive feats of bravery aside," she said, tilting her head slightly over one shoulder. "You were the one who requested we pursue this case. Allie and Max Jr. are here now. And I know that's on your mind, as well. Which means you're under a lot of pressure all around. Not to mention, as the TCD explosives expert, you've been taking lead on this. So let me ask again. All pretenses aside, and please be frank. We've known one another long enough for you to know I don't need or like my answers sugarcoated. Tell me friend to friend. How are you really doing?"

Max worked his jaw, deciding what and how much to say. Alana was a friend, but she was still his boss. The one who'd recruited him. The one who had his back, but also the one who handed him his backside as needed. "All right," he said, stretching his legs beneath the table. "Facing the bomb was tough. Tougher than I'd expected. A good example of theory versus reality. In theory, I knew what to do and was ready to do it. In reality, I nearly froze. I felt the panic rising before I'd even entered the building. And I wasn't convinced I could do the job once I was inside. Then I found the bomb, and part of me wanted to leave. The people were out. Their pets had been moved to safety. The only thing left in danger was an old, poorly maintained building."

Alana waited while he struggled to find words for his racing thoughts.

He kneaded his hands on the table, working to hold her eye contact, though his gaze darted away on its own more than once. "I couldn't let him damage the building. The apartments are people's homes. The residents were forced to leave everything behind when they evacuated. Their necessities, personal things, photos, mementos. Not to mention their security and peace of mind. Many of them likely had nowhere else to go." He paused to wet his lips, feeling another fact fall to his tongue. "And I wanted Fritz O'Lear to know who he was dealing with. I didn't want him to think he'd won. Or that he could win. Not by any measure."

She shifted, uncrossing and recrossing her legs. "And now?" she asked.

"Now I'm concerned he saw my interference as a challenge, and that instead of intimidating him, I provoked him. I'm worried something else will explode at any minute, this time taking lives in the process."

"Well, I'm not worried," she said, confidently. "I knew you were the best when I asked you to join my team, and I'm more sure of that today than ever. You've never let me down before. So there is no precedent to expect any differently in the future."

Warmed by her words, he felt his cheeks twitch as he fought a smile. "No precedent, huh?"

"None."

He released his grip on his hands and let them fall to his sides, shaking them out at the wrists.

"Have you been able to talk with Allie since your arrival?" Alana asked. "Better yet, tell me you've had a chance to kiss that chubby-cheeked son of yours."

"I have," he said, answering both her questions at once. "Allie and Max Jr. are both doing well."

"Excellent." Alana nodded in approval. "Well, I can see you're just fine, as expected. I suppose I'd better go and meet with the who's who and get back to Traverse City before that snake, Jenkins, makes another play for my job while I'm not there to keep a heel on him."

Max chuckled. "You'd think he'd be smarter than to mess with you."

She stretched to her feet and collected her things, a small smile on her lips. "You'd think." She offered her hand in a gentle shake as she passed.

Max held on to her a beat longer than necessary and gave her fingers a soft squeeze before releasing them. "Thank you for coming here, Alana. Your confidence means a lot."

A bloom of pride colored her cheeks. "You've got this, Max. I have no doubt Grand Rapids is in excellent hands. If you need anything, let me know."

ON LESS THAN two hours of sleep and far too much caffeine, Opaline donned her favorite eyelashes, then loaded up on lavender eye shadow and matching lip gloss in preparation for the morning meeting. She'd risen with the sun and gone to the office early, eager to share her new leads.

"Good morning!" she trilled at the sight of her teammates. "Hope you all got a little sleep last night."

A collective grumble rolled through the conference room on-screen. They'd clearly had as little rest as Opaline, but also not as much coffee.

Surprisingly, the teammate who normally looked the most fatigued seemed the most awake. She smiled at Max, wondering if his fresh-faced look had anything to do with his ex-wife arriving at the site of yesterday's bomb scare.

"Why don't we get started," Axel said, lifting a

hand toward the camera. He'd worn his usual dark dress pants, white dress shirt and tie. His hair was mussed and damp, likely from a recent shower, and when he raised his hand to run his fingers through the fair locks, his biceps were quite impressive. Axel Morrow was sexy and single, but the heavy dose of brotherly chemistry between him and Opaline stopped her thoughts on the matter right there.

But what was this? Opaline felt her brows rise. Her sister's gaze was fixed on their supervisor, too. Selena's eyes were dark, her lips parted, and there was something about the color in her cheeks. Dear sis had noticed the bod on their supervisory agent for this assignment, as well, and there was nothing sisterly about the way she was staring.

"We sent updates as they came available," Axel went on.

Selena turned her eyes back to the screen, completely in the zone.

Opaline reconsidered what she'd seen. Maybe she'd misread her sister's previous expression. It wouldn't be the first time or a surprise. She and Selena had been at odds so long she barely felt connected to her these days, beyond the thread of mutual frustration.

"A number of details and photos were sent from our search of O'Lear's apartment," Axel said. "We need to compile the data into one quick-view document for ease and convenience of access."

"I can do that," Opaline said. "I'm also running scans on bar codes I pulled from the images of the discarded pressure-cooker boxes. I'm hoping to use those numbers to determine where they were purchased. Same with the Tannerite. Maybe someone at one of those stores will remember something useful about our bomber. I'm still trying to track down info on his burner phone, but that's been slow."

Axel nodded. "Excellent. We've officially moved into manhunt mode. There's no question in my mind that Fritz O'Lear is our guy. The goal now is to find him before he strikes again." Axel's expression was hopeful as he looked into the camera. "Tell me you've got something we can run with today."

"I do," she said proudly. "I'm sending the overview now." She sat taller and launched the group email she'd set up before the call began.

The team reached for their phones.

"From the top," Opaline began. "I found a man named Mark Waters, who called himself O'Lear's lifelong friend. Bad news—the guy was in a fatal motorcycle accident about ten months ago. Good news—Waters's parents still live in Grand Rapids. I sent you their address and contact information. If O'Lear was truly a lifelong friend of their son, chances are they will remember him."

"Nice," Axel said. "Who's got this interview?"

Carly lifted her pen. "I'll go."

Axel nodded. "Take Aria."

The two women exchanged nods.

"Also," Opaline continued, "when I ran Mark Waters through the system, I found a car title in his name. Since he's not driving it, and was on a motorcycle when he passed, I'm guessing the car is either in storage or the new owner hasn't taken the time to transfer the title." She pursed her lips and waited.

"Maybe O'Lear is using it," Aria said. "We'll ask the family."

"Good work," Axel told Opaline. "Anything else?"

"I pulled up the names and contact information for three families who purchased homes from O'Lear when he worked for Ramsey Realty," she said.

"Who is Pamela Berry?" Max asked, obviously skipping ahead on the file Opaline sent.

Opaline grinned. That was her biggest news. "Pamela is Fritz O'Lear's high school sweetheart, and according to her Facebook account, he's someone she still sees from time to time."

A slick smile spread over Max's face. "I've got the girlfriend."

Selena's eyes widened and locked on Max. "I want in on that interview."

"Done," he agreed.

Opaline beamed. "The most recent selfies of Pamela with O'Lear were taken at pool halls or bowling alleys in town, which fits well with the hobbies list I gave you yesterday."

"We're on it," Max said.

Opaline smiled back. "Keep me in the loop. I'll try to locate the suspect while you all go on interviews."

"Do we have a description on that car?" Carly asked.

"Yes." Opaline switched screens, seeking and finding the details. "Beige, 1999, Toyota Camry. I can send a photo of Mark Waters with the vehicle about three years ago. It's not the clearest image of the car, but it's not the worst."

"Thanks," Carly said.

"Plate number?" Aria asked.

Opaline scanned the screen, then rattled off the information.

Max set his phone aside and turned to Rihanna, dutifully tapping away at her phone while the team made plans for the day's investigation.

She looked up and caught his eye. "Yes?"

"Can you get that vehicle description and plate number to the local PD?" Max asked. "Request officers and traffic cams begin looking for it. If Fritz is behind the wheel, we can track and capture him."

Rihanna wiggled her phone in one hand. "Already on it."

"Nice." He gave an approving nod.

Opaline felt her ever hopeful heart grow impossibly lighter. She'd provided leads that got the team energized. She'd boosted her friends' spirits, and the positive vibes flowing through her screen were her drug of choice.

"Anything else?" Max asked.

"That's all for now," she answered. "I'll be in touch as new information comes available."

"Thanks, Opaline," Max said, stretching upright. He pocketed his phone and threaded his arms into a black wool coat. "I think it's time I get to know Pamela Berry."

"Yes." Selena rose and collected her jacket, as well. She looked into the camera with a small, be-grudging smile. Proud, but frustrated. "Good job, Opaline."

"Thanks." Opaline held her breath as she dis-connected, and went out on the high note.

Chapter Seventeen

Max moved around the table to Selena as the others broke into groups, plotting their next steps.

Rihanna slipped out of the room immediately. Back to coordinating TCD efforts with local PD and media.

Selena tracked Max with her gaze, brows furrowed. "I hope you got some sleep last night. Some of us were concerned when we didn't hear from you."

"I did," he said, guilt tugging at him once more. "I came in a little early to review the information sent during the night. I think I've got a good handle on everything."

"Okay," she said. "For what it's worth, I'm glad you took the night for yourself. We need you sharp, so stop feeling guilty." She smiled. "It's written all over your face. Knock it off, McRay."

Max groaned. She'd known exactly how he'd been feeling. And if Selena had noticed, so had everyone else on the team. *Hazard of working with a group of federal agents*, he thought.

"Do you have any questions about the images and information we sent from O'Lear's apartment?" Selena asked.

"No, but I wouldn't mind taking a look at the place later. Being in his space might help me get a feel for who this guy is," Max said. "I'd like to see the evidence you brought in, too. Photos are fine. In person is better."

"Sounds good." Selena swept sleek dark hair off her shoulders, then shrugged into her coat. "We can hit the evidence room on our way out."

Max moved toward the door with his partner for the day, eager to get a look at everything taken out of O'Lear's apartment. "The pictures made it look like there weren't many materials left in the footlocker."

"There weren't," Selena agreed, pausing to tie the belt on her coat. "Lots of empty boxes."

"Makes me think the next bomb has already been made," Max said. "I'd kind of hoped you'd turn up the next device and bring it in, or all the materials to make it. Then we'd know he was stopped, at least temporarily. We could've kept watch at local stores, assuming he'd be on the hunt to purchase more."

"That would have been better."

Max frowned. "Yeah. Now we can't be sure if he's already made another device or not."

"So we'd better get moving," she said.

Axel reached the door first, phone in hand. He glanced at Max and Selena as he dialed. "I'm calling the local Department of Transportation to see if I can get someone to review traffic-cam footage from a three-block radius around the known bomb sites. Rihanna requested cops and cams watch for the Toyota moving forward, but I think it's worth looking backward, as well. Excuse me." He slipped into the hallway and out of sight.

Carly palmed her keys and caught the closing door. "Aria and I will go see what Mark Waters's family knows about O'Lear and their son's car. If we can confirm who has the vehicle, we'll let you know."

"Sounds good," Max said. "Stay in touch. I've got a bad feeling about the text O'Lear sent yesterday. We've pushed him, and he'll be out to punish us."

The team traded weary looks.

Carly circled a finger in a roundup motion. "Well, let's move out."

Max held the door for Selena, following Aria and Carly into the hallway. He and Selena took a look at the evidence confiscated from O'Lear's apartment before heading out in search of Pamela Berry.

Selena strode ahead of him into the lot. "Care if I drive?"

Max lifted his hands. "Nah, but I'm starting to feel like Miss Daisy. Axel drove me around all day when we went out together."

"Yeah, well, Aria drove me," Selena said, looking a little pale with the words.

Max chuckled. The rookie agent's driving had frightened more than one of his teammates so far, but Max, thankfully, hadn't had the pleasure.

"She is a terror behind the wheel. I'm not kidding. She took some turns that had me clutching my pearls."

Max climbed into the passenger seat, secretly thankful for Selena's offer to drive. He needed a few more minutes to think before jumping mentally into the day. His mind was still on Allie and how much he'd hated to leave her this morning. He hoped she wouldn't spend the day getting in her own head about what had happened between them last night, because it wasn't a mistake. Not for him. In fact, he hoped it was the first step on their path to finding their way back together. Permanently.

He'd kept himself from telling her he loved her, last night and again when he left this morning, but he already regretted the missed opportunities. She didn't want him to keep things like that from her again, and he understood the importance of being open with one another about what they were feeling, but this was different. When he'd held back on personal transparency during their marriage, it had been because he didn't want to think about how he felt or why he behaved the way he did. This time, he simply hadn't wanted to scare her off, and something told him that taking it slow right now would help rebuild her trust. He needed her to believe he was taking this seriously. Not rushing in.

Selena cast a number of curious looks in his direction as she drove, but it was several minutes before she finally spoke. "Have you dug into this woman's social-media profile? Opaline didn't give us a lot of personal details to go on. We could use the information to decide our best approach for this interview."

Max nodded, then kicked himself for not having done that already. A couple of feds showing up on Pamela's doorstep at breakfast could put her off. "Good call. I'll check that out."

He used his phone to search for Pamela Berry, then navigated to the only profile by that name in Grand Rapids. "Her bio says she has an associate's degree from Grand Rapids Community College. Looks like she just celebrated her thirty-sixth birthday," he said, describing everything that caught his attention as he scrolled. "She's platinum blonde with dark roots. Thin in the extreme. Extremely tan in the Christmas photos taken last month. Long hair." He flipped through several more shots before commenting again. "She's either dressing a little young for her age or trying to look high-fashion on a serious budget. She's got a couple candid photos of her with a birthday cake in a medical office setting. Plain clothes, not scrubs. I'm guessing she has an administrative position."

"So there's nothing in there to indicate she's unreasonable or has a bias against law enforcement?" Selena asked.

"No." Max breathed a little easier for that. Interviewing individuals with a grudge against the police made it more difficult to get straight answers. Everyone in America today seemed to have a strong opinion on law enforcement, one way or the other. Hopefully, Pamela was on the side that trusted and respected what he and his team were doing. Or at least preferred them to her ex. Otherwise, their best link to O'Lear would become another dead end.

Selena hit her turn signal and cruised into a gas station. "We're getting low on fuel, and I don't want to have to stop later if we get into something good." She pulled up to a pump, then settled the engine. "Be right back."

Max knew better than to offer to pump for her, despite the ridiculous temperature and snow on everything in sight. Selena and Aria had both shut him down for acts of chivalry in the past, making their preference for equality on the job crystal clear. Though the minute the workday ended, neither of them would've passed up the opportunity to stay warm in the SUV while he froze his other leg off in the cold. Carly, on the other hand, welcomed any act or offer of kindness by anyone at any time.

Thinking of kindness sent Max's mind back to Allie, and he dialed her number. He'd forgotten to ask her to stay home from the mall again today. Part of him said that staying home should be assumed, but the rest of him remembered what his mama used to say about assuming things. Plus, he wanted to hear Allie's voice and know she was okay. A gnawing feeling that trouble was coming hit him hard as he pressed Call.

"Max?" Allie answered on the first ring, a thread of fear in her voice. "Everything okay?"

"Yeah." He smiled, glad her fear was only born of concern for him and nothing more. "I'm calling for a favor," he said. "I need you to do something for me. I wouldn't ask if it wasn't important."

"I'm only going into the mall for five minutes today," she said, in her all-knowing way. "My parents are taking Max Jr. out for a day on the town, and I'm going to see how many online orders I can fill with no distractions. I'm hoping it will keep my mind off worrying about you."

"Only five minutes at the mall?" he clarified.

"Yep. I'm running in to grab a few things I left in the kiosk. Then I'll be working from home the rest of the day."

"Thank you." A wave of relief swept over him. "We're close to getting this guy now, I promise. You won't have to stay away from the mall much longer."

"Good, because I can't," she said. "The lease on that kiosk requires more sales than I make online."

"I know," Max admitted, "and I'll help you out however you need as soon as this is over. Until then, knowing you and Max Jr. are safe will help me concentrate so I can get this done."

"Fine."

He could practically hear her smile in the response.

"I appreciate you for doing this for me," he said.

"And I appreciate being given a choice instead of an order," she replied dryly. "So we're both having a good day."

Max laughed. "I guess we are."

"Now hurry up and catch the bad guy. Then come home to me."

His chest puffed with pride over the progress they were making. And her confidence filled him with everything he didn't know he needed. "Baby, there is nowhere else I'd rather be."

He said goodbye and disconnected with Allie as Selena returned to the driver's side.

She set a disposable cup of coffee in each of the two cupholders, then placed a white paper bag on the console between them while she buckled up. "They sold Krispy Kremes in there," she said, her expression caught somewhere between guilt and excitement. "I bought two. Be the partner I need right now and eat one so I don't eat them both."

Max grinned. "A doughnut and coffee on the job. I've never felt like more of a lawman than I do right now." He opened the bag and offered it to her first.

Selena tapped her doughnut to his before taking a bite. She moaned with satisfaction, then finished half before starting the SUV's engine. "Okay, now I'm ready."

Max smiled. "Let's start with the medical office where Pamela works instead of her home. We're closer to the office, and we can always head to her house from there if she has the day off."

"Agreed." Selena sipped her coffee, before shifting into gear. "Address?"

Max entered the name of the small family practice from Pamela's photo into a search engine, then tapped the address into the dashboard GPS.

It was time to catch the bad guy so Max could get home to his family.

Chapter Eighteen

Carly parked the SUV on a curving asphalt drive-way outside a stately brick home in an upscale gated community. Two large stone pillars stood on either side of the property's entrance. A house number was carved into one pillar. The name Waters was carved into the other.

"Wow," Aria said, unfastening her safety belt and turning to stare through her window. "I think my entire extended family could live in that house, and there are thirty-five of us in Traverse City alone."

"I don't know. That's a lot of Italians," Carly said, enjoying the look on Aria's face. Not awe, exactly—more like she might actually be calculating the available square feet per family member. Before she got too caught up in that, Carly delivered the bad news. "There's probably only one kitchen."

Aria laughed, spell broken. "You got me there. My aunts and grandma would kill each other." She climbed out and buttoned her coat to the top.

"Not your mom?" Carly asked, locking up and meeting Aria at the front of the vehicle.

"Nah. My mom would be cleaning something and protesting the arguments. Bless her, but she wants to be the voice of reason in a family who'd debate the sky was blue if you challenged them."

Carly laughed. It was hard to imagine growing up surrounded by family the way Aria had been. But it would've been interesting. "Well, the sky is definitely not blue today," she said, rolling her gaze heavenward. The dreary January day was gray from top to bottom. Gray clouds overhead. Dirty gray snow everywhere else.

The agents moved onto the massive front porch of the sprawling colonial home and stood beneath a giant wrought iron lantern. Carly rang the bell.

Aria leaned back, craning her neck for a scan along the snow-covered landscaping. "You think this looks like the kind of house where a kid who'd grow up with Fritz O'Lear lived? I pegged O'Lear for a broken-home, blue-collar family. How would he ever cross paths with a kid from this neighborhood?"

Carly pulled her lips to the side. It was an excellent question. Opaline hadn't been able to find O'Lear's parents yet, but the process wasn't always cut-and-dried. Maybe Fritz had a different last name than his parents. He could've run away and changed his, or maybe their names were never the same. Anything was possible, and despite her online sleuthing skills, Opaline was still working to locate his birth certificate, which would have made the task much easier. If they'd had any money, odds were that he wouldn't have lived in that run-down apartment building. "Hopefully we'll soon find out."

The door opened, and a petite woman in black dress slacks, a red blouse and diamond earrings looked out. She had fire-red hair and heels, nails and lips. Her eyes were green, like the cat who lived outside Carly's condo. Hopefully, the lady was nicer.

"Hello." She smiled politely, curiosity tugging her tightly Botoxed brow. Opaline had included an image of Mark Waters's parents, and this was definitely his mom.

Aria lifted her badge. "Hello, Mrs. Waters. I'm FBI special agent Calletti. This is Special Agent Welsh. We'd like to ask you a few questions about someone you might know. May we come in?"

The woman's artificially inflated lips opened and closed. "Well, yes. I suppose." She shuffled back a few steps, allowing room for them to enter.

"Thank you," Carly said softly, taking over where Aria had begun. "We won't keep you long. We're just looking for information on a man named Fritz O'Lear. We believe he was a friend of your son Mark's."

The older woman's eyes misted and her face flushed. She stood taller, likely attempting to remain in control of the unexpected emotion.

Carly knew grief when she saw it, and her heart broke immediately for the mother before her.

"Mark's been gone almost a year now."

"We know," Carly said, a little softer. "We're deeply sorry for your loss. We wouldn't bring up such a tender subject if it wasn't absolutely necessary. Would you like to sit down while we talk?"

Mrs. Waters fished a tissue from the box on a side table, then ushered them down a marble-floored hallway. One side of the space was lined in windows overlooking a snow-covered patio and garden, complete with stone statues and a large empty fountain. Carly assumed it was an extraordinary view in better weather. The opposite side of the hallway had wainscoting and a chair rail, above which hung a row of floral paintings in ornate, gilded frames. The hallway spilled into a vast gourmet kitchen. More windows. More fancy everything. Granite counters, an elaborate tile backsplash, cherry cabinets, top-of-the-line appliances and about two miles of kitchen island.

A balding man in a polo shirt and Dockers pulled a set of half-glasses down the bridge of his nose as Carly and Aria followed Mrs. Waters into the room. "Annie?"

Mrs. Waters went to the man's side. "Darling, these women are with the FBI, and they want to talk to us about Mark."

The man paled but extended an arm across the island. "Anthony Waters. What's this about?"

Aria took his hand first. "Special Agent Calletti. This is Special Agent Welsh."

"You can call me Carly," Carly said, accepting the man's hand for a shake. "We'd like to see if you remember a man named Fritz O'Lear. We believe he was connected to your son, Mark, and we'd like to know more about him. We're running thin on ways to do that."

The Waterses exchanged a troubled look.

Aria leaned against the island, separating the agents from the homeowners. "An older entry on your son's Facebook page referred to O'Lear as a lifelong friend. We hoped you might know him."

The couple shook their heads.

"Marky had a lot of friends," Mrs. Waters said. "Can I get you something to drink?" She switched her attention from Carly to Aria, then back. "I can make tea? Or coffee? I have bottled waters and juices."

"No, thank you, Mrs. Waters," Carly said. She brought up the images of O'Lear on her phone and passed the device to Mr. Waters. "Does he look familiar to you at all?"

Mr. Waters pushed the glasses back up the bridge of his nose. "Not this guy," he said, poking the more recent photo. The image changed, and the man's gaze jumped to Carly. "Sorry. I did something to it."

"No, it's fine." She pointed back to the screen. "This is another image we wanted you to see. Do you recognize him?" The image of O'Lear all shined up for Ramsey Realty centered the screen.

"Hmm." Mr. Waters took a longer look. "Maybe this man. Annie?" He handed the device to his wife, who'd already put on her glasses.

She drew the phone close and frowned. "I think I might. He looks incredibly familiar. I don't recall his name."

"Fritz O'Lear," Aria supplied. "Your son called him a lifelong friend."

Mrs. Waters returned the phone to Carly, biting her round bottom lip. "Maybe." She looked to her husband. "It's been years, but could that have been the name of Doris's little boy?"

"Who?" he asked, looking genuinely confused.

"Doris," she repeated. "She cleaned for me for several years after we moved here. Marky was young and still attending St. Joan of Arc school."

Her husband looked to the ceiling a moment, then back to his wife. "I don't remember Doris. How would I know her little boy?"

"He came with her sometimes," Mrs. Waters pressed, sounding more sure of herself by the moment. "When we had parties, she'd come on the weekends to clean up afterward, and she had to bring her son because she wasn't married. No family in town. No school on the weekend."

Mr. Waters listened, considered, looked to Carly, then shrugged. "She would know. I barely remember those days. I worked eighty hours a week back then. I was lucky to attend my own parties."

Carly forced a tight smile. "I understand." She moved her gaze to Mrs. Waters. "What happened to Doris? Any chance you have contact information for her now?"

"Or before," Aria said. "We're glad to work with anything you can offer. The matter is time-sensitive."

Mrs. Waters's expression fell. "I'm sorry, but no." She stepped closer, pressing her middle against the island between them. "Doris stopped cleaning for me when she got sick. I heard later from some of my friends who'd used her, too, that she didn't make it. Cancer." She whispered the final word.

"Did Doris work for a cleaning agency?" Aria asked.

Mrs. Waters shook her head. "She walked door-to-door one spring. She had her son with her. He had a little bike with training wheels. She put paper flyers in the mailboxes, offering spring cleaning. She did such a nice job that a lot of us hired her to come back regularly."

Aria's shoulders slumped.

Carly kept her warm smile in place. Hoping this wasn't another dead end. "Do you remember anything about her little boy? It sounded as if your son kept in touch with him after the loss of his mother."

Mrs. Waters shifted, and her gaze darted away briefly. "No. We never saw the boy outside the times he came with Doris to clean," she said, "but it's possible he and Mark saw each other again. The truth is that Mark had some troubles in high school, and we didn't get to meet a lot of his friends."

"Got kicked out of St. Joan of Arc for using pot," Mr. Waters said, his voice going hard and gravelly. "Don't let her sugarcoat it for you just because he's gone. Mark was caught drinking here more times than we could count, and that was before he was old enough to drive. He was busted with pot at his over-priced private school. He blew off college. Moved out at eighteen and didn't look back. He showed up here from time to time, mostly when he needed money. The next thing we know, there are highway patrolmen on our doorstep at three a.m. telling us he crashed a motorcycle going a hundred miles an hour in the rain." He tore his glasses off and tossed them onto the countertop. "That's what I know about my son. I don't know anything about who he did or didn't call a friend. What do you want this guy, O'Lear, for anyway?"

"Serial bombing," Aria said.

Mr. and Mrs. Waters's eyes widened a moment before Mr. Waters cursed. "I'm going to the study. Good luck, Detectives." He headed for an ornately carved archway on the other side of the kitchen, then vanished through it.

Carly shot a look at Aria, whose mouth had pulled into a frown. They were special agents, not detectives, and the lack of success they'd been having on this case made that fact abundantly clear.

"Mrs. Waters," Aria said, turning a compassionate look on their hostess, who was still staring after her husband. "Just one more question, if you don't mind. Did you know your son owned a Toyota Camry when he passed?"

She stilled, turning her attention back to the agents. "We bought Mark a Camry when he turned eighteen. Before he moved out. We wanted him to have a way to come home and visit after he left."

"Any idea where that car is now?" Aria asked.

"No." Mrs. Waters sucked in a ragged breath. "It was the last thing we bought him. We assumed he sold it for drugs or cash a long time ago. Maybe even that he traded it for the motorcycle he was on when he…" She pressed the tissue to her nose again. "I'm sorry. I just can't believe he's gone. There's so much I would do differently if I could."

Carly pulled a business card from her pocket and set it on the countertop. "We'll get out of your hair now. Please apologize to your husband for us, if we upset him. We're truly sorry to have put you through this today. If you think of anything later that you want to tell us, just give me a call."

"We can see ourselves out," Aria said.

Carly followed Aria back down the hall to the front door, then into the freezing winter day. They didn't speak again until they climbed into the SUV and cranked up the heat.

"Well, that was a bust," Aria said. "We upset those poor people for nothing."

"Yeah." Carly admired the big house another moment before backing down the drive and pulling away. "Hopefully Max and Selena are having better luck."

Aria sighed. "I can't see how they could be doing worse."

Carly's phone rang, and she recognized the number on-screen. She answered using the speaker option. "Hey, Axel," she said. "You've got me and Aria."

"Hey. How'd it go with the Waters family?" he asked. "Were you able to catch them at home?"

"Yep," Aria said. "Nice people. Total dead end."

"Their son was estranged at the time of his death,"

Carly explained. "They weren't familiar with his friends, and his mom didn't even realize he still had the Toyota. It was a gift from her and Mark's father when Mark was eighteen."

"So O'Lear could potentially be driving that car?" Axel asked.

"It's possible," Carly said. "Mrs. Waters thinks O'Lear might be the son of her former cleaning lady, Doris. Unfortunately, Doris passed away years ago, and according to Mrs. Waters, she didn't have any family other than her son."

Axel made a disgruntled sound. "So we know this guy's had it rough. Single mom. Potential feelings of abandonment by Dad. No father figure. Mom cleans for rich people in town, which could've led to being teased. Then Mom gets sick. Income stops. Medical bills pile up. She dies, and his anchor goes with her. Do we know how old he was when she passed?"

Carly shook her head. "No."

"So he was potentially orphaned," Axel continued. "That's a lot of weight for one kid. He's probably felt like an underdog his whole life. I'll see if Opaline can find any record of him in the foster system."

"Good call," Aria said. "Have you spoken with Max and Selena?"

"No. Not yet," Axel answered. "I'm going to reach out to them when I finish here. I've got O'Lear's face on a flyer, and I'm canvassing the neighborhood around his building. I have about a half dozen more apartments to go before I call it quits on this area and move to the block with Burger Mania."

"Learning anything?" Aria asked.

Axel gave a humorless laugh. "Most people don't answer their doors. The ones who do are a split. Some don't want to talk to me. The rest say they don't recognize O'Lear's picture. A couple of men on the sidewalk said they thought they knew him from some bar downtown. They had no idea he lived on this block."

Carly glanced at the phone on her outstretched palm. "Opaline said he and his ex-girlfriend liked to bowl and play pool. You can shoot pool at a lot of bars, and a lot of bowling alleys have bars and billiards."

"I guess I'll head downtown next instead," Axel said. "It'll be nice to get inside and warm up. I'll give Max a call when I'm finished at Shaky's Bar. You can tell by the name it's going to be a good one."

Aria laughed. "Sounds like someplace I'd find my brothers. Bad music. Dim lighting to hide decades of wear and tear, an awesome burger and about ninety beers on tap."

"I could go for a good burger right now," Axel said, wind whipping through his cell phone's speaker.

"You need any help over at Shaky's?" Carly asked. "Maybe we should rendezvous there for lunch."

"Yes," Aria answered. "Greasy burgers. Salty fries. I'm in. Tell Selena and Max."

"How's Max doing?" Carly asked. "Yesterday had

to be a tough one for him. Then he didn't respond to any of our messages last night."

"I think he's just fine," Axel said, a peculiar lilt to the words.

"You think?" Carly rolled the words and tone around in her mind. "Oh," she said. "So he wasn't at the hotel when you got back, then?"

"Nope."

"And he wasn't there when you got up for work this morning either?" she asked, trading grins with Aria as the facts set in.

"Nope."

Carly felt her smile widen. Max had gone to see his ex-wife and son for dinner, and he'd stayed the night. "I guess you're right. He's doing just fine."

Chapter Nineteen

Grand Rapids Family Practice was housed in a squat one-story brick building near downtown. Max held the door for Selena as they entered the small medical office. According to the website, GRFP had four full-time doctors and a handful of regular staff. Currently, they also had a mostly empty parking lot and a completely empty waiting room.

Mauve-and-green padded chairs lined the waiting-area walls, interspersed with small rectangular tables. A hodgepodge of picture books and popular magazines topped the tables, and there was an indestructible-looking, topless toy box against one wall.

They crossed the silent space to the check-in desk and smiled politely at the woman on the other side.

"Hello," Selena greeted the platinum blonde behind the desk. The woman's name badge identified her as Pamela, but Max didn't need that to recognize her. She looked exactly like all her photos on Facebook.

"Good morning," she answered. "How can I help you?"

Selena raised her badge, giving Pamela a serious look before tucking the identification away. "We're hoping to have a word with you. Is there somewhere we can talk privately?"

A second woman stalled as she passed by, apparently noting the distinct and sudden tension. "Is everything okay, Pamela?" she asked, coming to stand beside the seated woman.

"Yes. Fine," Pamela said. "Thank you."

The second woman wore pink scrubs, orthopedic shoes and had at least twenty years on the rest of them. She put her hands on her hips. "Then maybe I can help you," she suggested, fixing a warning look on Selena and Max.

"No." Pamela stood woodenly, then forced a bright smile. "I've got this. But can you cover for me? I'll only be a minute."

The older woman narrowed her eyes at Selena and then Max. "Okay." She unhooked the stethoscope from around her neck and lowered herself into Pamela's vacant seat. "Let me know if you need anything."

"Thank you." Pamela lifted a hand in goodbye, then went around to open the door separating the waiting area from the offices and exam rooms. "We can talk in the kitchen."

The area beyond the waiting room was like every other doctor's office Max had ever seen. Watered-down paint colors. A tall scale and height device pressed against a wall with coat hooks. Open exam-room doors with empty tables covered in paper. A

handful of men and women in colorful scrubs looking at open files as they buzzed around.

The office's kitchen was as simple as the rest
of the place. A countertop and sink on one wall. A
lunch table down the middle with plastic folding
chairs around it. Zero bells and whistles. A lami-
nated evacuation map taped above the sink.

Pamela shut the door once they were all inside.
She moved around to the kitchenette and leaned
against the small counter, knocking into a collection of assorted coffee mugs. Her khaki pants and
white sweater were snug on her lean frame, and she
wore trendy on-brand sneakers instead of the plain,
comfort-first footwear worn by the other staff they'd
passed in the hallway. "Is someone hurt?" she asked,
pushing a swath of platinum hair off her shoulder.

"No." Max offered her his hand. "I'm Special Agent
Max McRay. This is Special Agent Selena Lopez.
We'd like to ask you a few questions about a man we
think you know. His name is Fritz O'Lear."

"Fritz?" Pamela asked, swinging her gaze from
Max to Selena, then back. "And he isn't hurt?"

"No," Selena answered. "He's not hurt."

Max and Selena waited then, allowing Pamela
time to ask herself what the FBI wanted with her ex,
before moving forward. Max evaluated her expressions as she worked through the situation. Surprise.
Confusion. Concern.

"What do you want with Fritz?" she asked, crossing her arms and leaning away. Not a great pair of
body signals. She was putting up a barrier, then add-

ing additional space, though she could only manage an extra few inches from her position at the counter.

"We need to get in contact with him," Selena said, her silky voice adding a measure of calm to Pamela's visible tension. "Do you have any idea where he might be?"

Pamela shook her head. "I haven't seen Fritz since Christmas."

"Tell us about that," Max said, doing his best imitation of a tough guy. He hadn't gotten a good read on her yet and didn't want to give her the time to decide against being helpful. If the surprise of their appearance at Pamela's office was all they had going for him right now, he needed to make the most of it.

She released a nervous breath. "I ran into Fritz at the bowling alley's holiday party a few days before Christmas." She ran her hand up and down one bicep, but didn't uncross her arms. "We played a couple games of pool. Had some drinks." She smiled. "There was a lot of mistletoe and nostalgia, so I invited him back to my place for the night." Her cheeks pinkened at the admission. "The holidays are a confusing time. It's easy to feel lonely. And I've known him for years."

"How did he seem that night?" Selena asked. "Was he upset about anything in particular?"

Pamela's brows arched. "A little." She chewed her lips, choosing her words. "Before he left, he told me he's always regretted we didn't end up together, and he thought maybe we could have a second chance."

"And?" Selena asked.

Pamela wrinkled her nose. She looked at her shoes, then her pale blue fingernail polish. "I laughed at him." She raised her eyes again, looking the way Max might if he'd accidentally kicked a small puppy. "I told him what we had was great for high school, but it ended for a reason, and that our one-night stand was only that. We remind each other of when we were young and fearless. Then got carried away. Nothing more."

Selena gave an understanding nod. "How'd he take that?"

"Not great. I tried to explain, but I think I made things worse the more I talked. I said he was romanticizing what had happened between us. It was a onetime adult hookup, and I barely remembered our monthlong high school romance. I told him those things aren't meant to last. Then I remembered he didn't date back then. In hindsight, I think those dates when we were teens, and the night after the bar, all meant more to him than me. I feel terrible for hurting him. Fritz has had it rough." She tucked a fingernail between her teeth and began to gnaw.

Max traded a pointed look with Selena. He hadn't known what to expect from Pamela before they spoke, but this wasn't it. She'd just described a third recent rejection for O'Lear. For someone already teetering on the edge of a mental break, and with little left to lose, it could've been enough to push him over the edge, especially after the Burger Mania employee's rejection and this one from Pamela. "Do you have any idea where Fritz could be now?" Max asked. "If you wanted to get ahold of him, where would you start?"

Pamela shrugged. "Have you checked his apartment? He doesn't go out much, and he's not working right now, or he wasn't at Christmas anyway, so you might catch him there. I have the address. I can write it down for you." She turned to collect a pen from the top of a small microwave, then froze. She turned back, looking a little greener. "You were at his place yesterday. I remember now." She pointed to Max. "You were the guy in the bomb suit. I watched you talking to the local police after you left the building. I was worried because I recognized Fritz's building."

Selena took the chair opposite Pamela. "Breathe."

Pamela made a small strangled sound.

Max crossed his arms and widened his stance behind Selena, running mentally through the possibility Pamela was next on O'Lear's hit list.

She looked from agent to agent. "Do you really think Fritz is the Grand Rapids bomber?"

"We know he is," Selena said gently. "And he knows we know."

Pamela gasped.

"He's hiding, and probably unhappy we stopped his attack yesterday," Selena said. "So it is imperative that we find and stop him before anyone else gets hurt."

Max stepped forward, then crouched before the table. "You said you see Fritz around sometimes.

But you haven't seen him since Christmas." Since she'd rejected him. "Is that common?"

She frowned. "I'm not sure. It's barely been a month, and there were holidays in between, but he wasn't at Shaky's for New Year's Eve." She wet her lips. "He hasn't missed that party in a decade, but I figured he was avoiding me. I knew I'd hurt his feelings, and I was hoping to apologize. I didn't get to."

"You don't have a phone number for him?" Selena pressed. They had one for the text he'd sent, but maybe he used another phone.

She nodded, then gave them the number they already knew.

Max cast a look in Selena's direction. "I can make some calls and get a safe house set up for her."

"What?" Pamela said, voice cracking with panic. "For me? You think he'd try to kill me? Because I didn't want to rekindle a high school relationship?"

Maybe, Max thought. *O'Lear has certainly killed for less*. He stretched onto his feet and liberated the phone from his pocket while Selena spoke with Pamela.

"We think he's been targeting people who've recently rejected him," Selena explained, as Max sent a series of update texts to Axel, Rihanna and the team.

"That doesn't make any sense," Pamela complained. "Fritz and I are friends."

"Is there anyone else he might have a beef with?" Selena asked. "We know he has at least one more attack planned, and we think that could happen at any time."

Pamela cried.

Axel and Rihanna both responded almost instantly to Max's text. Axel would have a safe house arranged through Grand Rapids PD. Rihanna had a cruiser on its way to collect Pamela and take her to the new destination.

"Pamela," Selena said. "I know this is upsetting, but can you think of anyone else Fritz was upset with? Did he mention someone specific the last time you saw him?"

"No." She batted confused, tear-filled eyes. "Maybe. I don't know. I can't think."

"Look," Selena said. "I know we've given you a lot to process, and you're probably feeling scared, betrayed and a little ambushed right now, but there are lives at stake, so I need you to be sure."

Max forwarded Axel's and Rihanna's texts to Selena, then went to join the women at the table.

Pamela stilled, brows furrowing. "There was someone. A guy from his old neighborhood works at Coffee Coven now."

Max lifted his phone once more. "What's his name? I'll get Grand Rapids PD to pick him up and protect him while we check out the lead."

"I don't know." Pamela shook her head. "Fritz thought the guy spit in his drink, and when he demanded to speak to the manager, the guy tapped his badge and laughed at him. I guess he was the manager. The whole exchange got the other workers laughing together behind the counter. There's a bunch of teens and college kids that work there these days. They're all obnoxious. I only go there because it's the best place for a latte in the entire mall."

Chapter Twenty

Allie turned off her blow-dryer and rubbed a towel over the steamy bathroom mirror, clearing the fog. She'd made a quick trip to the mall and set up a workstation in the kitchen before indulging in some long-overdue self-care. It wasn't often that her parents took Max Jr. for more than a couple of hours, mostly because Allie hated to be away from him, but today, she was eager for the time alone. Before she got to work, she wanted to bask in the afterglow of a perfect night with Max and dream about where that renewed connection might take them. Hopefully back to her bed. Maybe even back to the altar.

She'd stood beneath a stream of piping hot water, the volume on her radio cranked up to support her one-woman shower concert, and she'd stayed there until she'd shaved, shampooed and exfoliated every inch of herself. She stepped out feeling shiny, fresh and about five years younger.

Her hair had dried and swelled to twice its usual size under the heat and pressure of her dryer, a device she rarely had time for these days. The wild blond curls Max loved to run his fingers through were softly scented with her favorite apricot deep conditioner.

Allie opened the bathroom door to release the steam and better admire her work in the foggy mirror, then went into her adjoining bedroom to dress. She slid into her softest jeans and an olive-colored sweater that brought out the green in her hazel eyes.

She'd made a decision in the shower.

When Max came for dinner tonight, she would tell him exactly how she felt. Whatever had gone wrong in their marriage, she still loved him. She'd never stopped. And in hindsight, she was a contributing factor in their breakup. She'd played the victim at the time, wanting more from him than he could give, then tucking her tail and turning away when he didn't comply. In truth, she was no more a victim than Max. She was his wife, and she should have fought for him. She should have stayed and demanded he get the help he needed to ease his PTSD and stop burying himself in his work. The love he and Allie shared was bigger and stronger than any trauma, and she should've been beside him every time he entered and exited that counselor's office. Max had told her the other night that he'd abandoned her when she was his teammate, but she'd abandoned him, too. And she was ready to do what it took to make that up to him.

A soft creak caught her ear, somewhere outside her room, followed by the sound of footfalls on her hardwood floor.

She smiled with the realization her parents had stopped home for something. It wasn't unusual. They often popped in and out when they had Max Jr., grabbing an extra change of clothes, another blanket or toy. If they'd been shopping, they occasionally stopped in to show off their bounty before heading out again.

"Talk about perfect timing," she called, pressing small diamond stud earrings into her pierced lobes. "Tell me what you think of this sweater." She hurried out to catch her mom, but the home was silent as she padded down the hall.

The kitchen and living room were empty.

Allie turned in a small circle, gooseflesh crawling over her toasty warm skin. She scanned the rooms for signs her mom had dropped something off, or maybe picked something up, then left. Nothing seemed out of place.

Had she been wrong about the footfalls?

An icy chill swirled through the kitchen, forcing the back door open wide. The gust hit Allie in the face and chest, complete with flurries from the world outside.

She rushed toward the door, sliding in melted clumps of snow on her kitchen floor. Footprints, she realized, but her mother never used the back door.

No one did.

Fear-laced adrenaline shot through her limbs, and she lunged for the door, slamming it shut and twisting the lock. Then she ran for her bedroom. Allie grabbed her phone from the nightstand and stared in disbelief at the notification of seven missed calls from Max.

She'd been in the shower, been drying her hair.

She locked her bedroom door, creating a barrier against the intruder, then stifled a whimper as she fumbled to unlock the device with suddenly shaking hands. Either someone had been in her house, or they were still there now. She could only pray it wasn't the latter. Her thumbs moved woodenly over the screen as she mentally processed the possibility someone had been inside her home. Someone could still be inside her home. And wherever Max was, it was too far away to help.

A flash of blinding pain shot through her head without warning, pitching her forward and knocking the phone from her grip. Her palms and knees slammed against the floor. Her cell phone skittered into the doorjamb with a crack!

A sob broke on her lips, and a scream built in her chest. Confusion faded into pinpoint clarity, and Allie knew it was too late for anyone to help. A feral yell ripped from her core, leaving her throat burning and raw. She couldn't dial 911, but she could fight. Max had taught her how.

Allie rocked onto the balls of her feet, prepared to deflect her intruder, then make a run for help.

Instead, angry fingers curled deep into the back of her hair, hard fingernails scraping the skin of her scalp. With one thrust from her assailant's arm, Allie's forehead beat against the carpet, effectively stopping her flight.

Blood pooled in her mouth. Her tongue and lip throbbed, one bitten, the other busted as her face connected with the floor.

"Shhh," her assailant whispered into her ear. His heavy knee pressed against her spine, crushing her stomach into the rug beside her bed. "You don't want to do that," he warned. Hot tears fell from her eyes. His dank breath clung to her cheek as he spoke. "No fighting. No running. I have your family."

Allie sucked in a shallow, ragged breath. Her sobs instantly silenced. She waited, biting back the cries, desperate to know what he would say next, and prepared to comply.

"Attagirl," he said, easing his weight off her. "I've attached a bomb to your parents' little station wagon. They're taking your boy out for ice cream. You wouldn't want to see them all go boom, now, would you?"

Allie pressed her lips against the building sob. She shook her head. She would do as he said. Anything he said.

"Give me any trouble at all, and I'll dial the number that detonates that bomb," he promised. "Their safety depends on you. Understand?"

She nodded hard and fast, tears blurring her vision and the taste of blood turning her stomach.

He yanked her up by her hair, and she cried out unintentionally, shocked by the fresh jolt of pain and struggling to get her feet beneath her. "Move," he growled. "Now."

She stumbled forward as he shoved her into the hall, through the kitchen, then out into the snow.

He didn't have to tell her who he was. Allie already knew.

This was Fritz O'Lear. The Grand Rapids bomber. And he was going to kill her.

Chapter Twenty-One

Max breathed easier when he and the TCD arrived at Great Lakes Mall, the shopping center where Allie leased a kiosk, and found she wasn't there. It had only taken a few minutes of speaking with Emilio West, the Coffee Coven manager, to erase any doubt from Max's mind that he was the bomber's fourth target. Emilio had answered the phone when Max called, then ranted, complained and guffawed through a half dozen stories about how much he hated Fritz O'Lear.

According to Emilio, O'Lear had been a loner in school and a stalker of Pamela, before they dated and afterward. He claimed that O'Lear lurked on the outside of groups, often lingering near attractive women, attempting to flirt, but always failing. And allegedly visited the mall several times a week.

Emilio said O'Lear had a bad habit of coming into Coffee Coven to bother the young girls behind the counter. He made the baristas uncomfortable and held up the lines, so Emilio had told him to leave, loudly and often. And the last time O'Lear had been in for coffee, Emilio had incited the workers to laugh at him. He hadn't been back since.

Max dialed Allie once more as he walked the still escalator, back to the food court for a rendezvous with Axel. The squeak of gym shoes on tile floors told him another wave of exiting employees and shoppers was on the way out. Local PD had coordinated with mall security to evacuate the building. Meanwhile, Sergeant Sims was rounding up the bomb squad to help Max search.

Max's call, like all the others before it, went to voice mail.

Axel met him at the base of the unmoving steps, brows furrowed in concern. "Any luck?"

"No, but at least she isn't here."

"True." Axel bobbed his head, looking a bit relieved, as well. "The place is nearly emptied," Axel said. "We'll get started soon and be done before you know it. Then you can swing by and check on Allie yourself."

"It's a big mall," Max said, pulling his attention back to the job at hand. He liked the idea of checking on Allie in person, but it would take time to do a thorough job in a building this size. "It's a lot of ground to cover."

Fire and Rescue was on the way, along with multiple ambulances, in preparation for a worst-case scenario.

Max could only pray they were as lucky as the last time.

"Good news," Axel said. "When I expressed the

same concern to Chief Drees, he suggested we reach out to a local training center for search-and-rescue dogs. Grand Rapids PD has used their services to find missing people and locate bodies. There's also a team trained to find accelerants."

Max felt his mood lighten. "Nice." He'd worked with bomb-sniffing canines overseas, and their abilities were astounding. Nearly unbelievable.

"Rihanna gave the training center a call, and they're rallying a set of handlers and canines as we speak."

"That's good. The dogs will make short work of the search." Max pressed his fists to his hips and scanned the strangely off-putting scene. The bright neon signs and colorful food-court decor seemed unnatural in their silence. The tables and counters were empty. The individual eateries dark. Only the faint, peppy notes of music on a mall-wide sound system remained. Forgotten by whoever had been in charge. Leaving an eerie abandoned-carnival vibe to rival any childhood nightmare.

Axel's phone screen lit, and he turned it over to check the message. "We've got about twenty minutes on the canines," Axel said. "Looks like they're on their way. We can brief the handlers while they suit up before heading in."

"That works. Emilio said this was his afternoon to do payroll in the office instead of helping at the counter. My best guess is that O'Lear would try to hit him then, when he would be predictably immobile for a long period. Stuck at his desk pushing papers." Max angled away from Axel, discreetly checking his phone for messages.

"Have you tried Allie's parents?" Axel asked, knowing exactly what Max was up to. "They live right next door. If she isn't with them, they can at least run over and check on her to put your mind at ease. They can probably get it done while you're on the phone."

Max had considered the idea already but hadn't followed through with making the call. Allie would say he was overreacting, which she hated.

"Hey," Carly called, moving toward Max and Axel in long, determined strides.

Aria and Selena were on her heels.

"Media has arrived," Aria announced. "Local PD created a perimeter and are pushing evacuees to leave the lot. Most are dragging their feet. Wanting answers. Everyone's making calls. The whole city probably knows what's happening by now."

"City Planning delivered the most recent set of blueprints," Carly said. "We spread them out in the surveillance transport that Chief Drees arrived in. His men are taking a look now. I told him you'd be there soon to mark the search route."

"Thank you," Max said. "Let's take a look."

Axel lifted a finger on one hand, then pulled the cell phone from his pocket and frowned. "It's Chief Drees now." He swiped the screen. "Morrow."

Selena moved to Max's side, crossing her arms as she looked across the cavernous space. "Any ideas how you're going to tackle a place this size?"

"Some." He widened his stance and waited as Aria and Carly moved closer. "We'll break it into quadrants for efficiency and clear them one by one. Starting at Coffee Coven, then spreading out in an arch. We'll use two teams. One on each floor, both covering the same quadrant, then sweeping out. We want to make sure O'Lear didn't plant the device above his target, with the intent of collapsing a section of the building onto the shop."

"And we won't have to search the entire place," Aria said, casting a look at Max for an affirmative nod. "There wouldn't be a reason to plant a bomb in a maternity store or nail salon."

"True," Max said. "Knowing Emilio is the target and Coffee Coven is the scene of the perceived offense, we have a place to start. If we don't find the device there, we'll move to other key locations in Emilio's typical workday. Places O'Lear might have expected him to be at a specific time. Where he took breaks. Ate meals. Used the restroom. Shopped." Max would add those locations to the search plan when they went out to review the blueprints. "Same protocol for each area, searching both floors as we go. Honestly, I'll be surprised if O'Lear hadn't planned to go for him at the Coffee Coven office. So far, he's been very direct in his attacks."

"How big a blast are we talking?" Aria asked.

Max rolled his shoulders, attempting to relieve the building tension. "The devices O'Lear builds will create a fireball twenty feet wide. The projectiles packed inside with the Tannerite will move like shrapnel, through walls, through flesh and bone, traveling faster than the speed of sound and for more than a hundred yards. If you're nearby when the device detonates, you'll be injured before you've even heard the explosion, and the resulting shock wave will reach the buildings across the road, potentially to the end of the next block." He glanced back and forth as if he could find O'Lear lurking in a corner. "We have to move fast. If he's tipped off by news reports, he might pull the trigger sooner rather than later."

Aria rocked back on her heels, appropriately speechless.

"We've got a problem." Axel's projected voice turned the foursome around once more. His expression stole the oxygen from Max's lungs.

"What is it?" Carly asked.

Axel gripped the phone in one lowered hand, his knuckles nearly as white as his cheeks.

"The woman you spoke to earlier, Pamela Berry, is a leak," Axel said. "The team had her call Fritz and leave a voice mail, asking for him to call her back. We started tracking her cell-phone activity this morning after Opaline provided her information as a potential contact. Chief Drees says she didn't wait for O'Lear to call her back, but phoned him again and tipped him off."

Max cursed. "How the hell did that happen? Didn't they take her phone after she left the voice mail?"

"Apparently not fast enough," Aria said.

Selena frowned. "Why would she do that, tip him off?"

Axel rubbed his tired eyes, looking more agitated by the moment. "I don't know, but she apparently asked him point-blank if he was the Grand Rapids bomber. When he didn't answer, she started crying and begging him not to hurt anyone else. She mentioned you and Max by name. Also the mall, Coffee Coven and Emilio West. Then she begged O'Lear's forgiveness for whatever happened between them and told him not to bother trying to hurt her, because the FBI was sending her to a safe house. I guess she went on and on, telling him everything we absolutely didn't want him to know, until he hung up. Then she called her parents. Her sister. Her friends." Axel stopped to draw in a long, aggravated breath before releasing it with a fresh scowl.

"Well, that explains how the media got here before the building was even empty," Aria said.

Axel groaned. "She's either a truly emotional wreck, too far gone to realize the damage she's doing, or she's a drama junkie seeking a spotlight. Either way, she's blown the whistle."

Max scrubbed a hand over his face. "I did not see that coming." He laced his fingers on top of his head and paced. O'Lear had a heads-up. So what was his next move? "The bomb is either already here, or it isn't. If it isn't, he's not getting in here now."

Aria inched toward the massive two-story windows along the front entrance. "He's going to be mad we've interfered again. If the bomb's here, he could detonate early, like you said. Wait until he thinks you're near, then press the button. Is it even safe to search now?"

Selena joined Aria at the glass. "What if we reach out to one of the news channels?" she suggested. "We could ask them to quietly pan the crowds for him or the Toyota. Maybe he's here, and we can get him into custody before the search."

Max considered the option. "That could help. Without O'Lear, our chances of a safe search and seizure increase. I don't like the thought of him out there, waiting. Luring us close enough for maximum damage."

"On it," Carly said. "I'll call Rihanna to place the request."

Selena nodded. "Thanks."

Max let the plan settle in. They'd already decided O'Lear liked to watch, so it was reasonable to think he might be nearby. "Until Pamela called him, he probably assumed he still had some measure of invincibility. He knew we had his name, image and address, but not his whereabouts. It probably seemed to him like he still had the upper hand. After Pamela called, things changed. He knew he'd been caught and we were closing in."

"Which is an emotional rush in itself," Carly said. "There's a freedom in being this close to arrested. He'll feel as if he can do anything because the worst has already happened. He's been found out, and he will go to jail. He's got nothing left to lose."

Axel's phone lit, and he lifted it to check the new notification. "Opaline."

Max checked his watch while Axel read the text. With a little luck, the canines and handlers would be ready to work soon. Max was eager to get over to Allie's place.

"Max." The word was hard on Axel's tongue.

"What?" Max froze, certain something terrible had happened.

Had another bomb gone off? Was Max wrong about the final target?

"Traffic cams got a hit on that Camry," Axel said. "And a clear shot of O'Lear behind the wheel."

Max's gaze snapped back to the windows. "Is he here?"

"The footage is from last night," Axel warned. "Outside our hotel."

Max narrowed his eyes. "Damn it!" They'd evacuated the wrong building. "Call Rihanna. We need a team over there to get those people out. Can we redirect the canines and handlers?"

There were hundreds of rooms at the hotel. A wedding party had checked in last night as Max had headed out. Families. Children. The potential casualties were at least double that of the apartment building.

"Max," Axel warned. "The Camry followed you to a bakery, then a shop on Main Street. We lost track of both vehicles when you reached the residential area east of downtown."

Max's vision tunneled and his ears rang. O'Lear

hadn't targeted the hotel. "He followed me to Allie's."

"Give her another call," Axel suggested, lifting his phone to his ear. "He followed you last night, but you've spoken with Allie a few times today, and she's been fine. I'm going to send a cruiser to check on things. I'll ask the officer to report back, then stay out front until we can wrap this up and get over there."

Max nodded, torn between leaving the mall to check on Allie immediately and beginning the search on his own, to save some time, so he could get to Allie's as soon as possible. He was leaning toward the former when his phone rang. "It's Allie's mom."

"Hello? Mrs. Fedder?" he asked. "Is everything okay?"

"No," his former mother-in-law cried. "She's gone. I called the police. They said someone is on the way, but I don't know what to do."

"What do you mean she's gone?" Max demanded. "When? How?"

Axel pried Max's hand and phone away from his ear, then tapped the speaker option on the screen. "You're now with the TCD, Mrs. Fedder. What details can you give us about the situation?"

Panic raced in Max's heart and limbs. "Max Jr.?" he asked, suddenly realizing he wasn't sure when his ex-wife went missing or if their son was with her.

"He's with us," she answered, regaining herself slightly. "We took him out so Allie could work. The back door was open when we brought him home.

There's snow in the kitchen. There's blood on the bedroom carpet."

The team's phones buzzed and dinged around Max as rage and remorse circled in his gut. His worst nightmare had come true. He'd brought danger into Allie's life. O'Lear wanted to hurt him, and he'd known exactly how to get the job done.

"Max," Axel said, turning his phone to show the message just received.

You took something important to me. Now I'm taking something important from you.

Beneath the horrific words was a photo of Allie. With a bomb around her neck.

Chapter Twenty-Two

Allie opened her eyes slowly, fighting the pain in her head and the blur of her vision. Her muddled thoughts scrambled to process an unusual scent. The hard, cold slab beneath her and the unfamiliar touch against her throat.

Slowly, the strange smell registered. Disinfectant. And her eyes, open as far as she could manage, came into focus, along with the memories of her predicament. She was on the floor, not her bed, in what seemed to be a janitor's closet. A large yellow wheeled bucket stood across from her in the small space, a mop handle sprouting from within.

Allie moaned, and her eyelids fluttered open once more, though she hadn't recalled closing them. And Fritz O'Lear came into view.

She gasped at the rush of memories, now plowing through her like a freight train.

She'd been abducted by the Grand Rapids bomber. He'd taken her from her home. She'd gone willingly to protect her family from a bomb he'd somehow left with them. Then he'd hit her from behind as she slid onto the back seat of his car. "Where are we?" she croaked, her throat dry and tight. "What are you doing?"

O'Lear moved closer, lowering to her side, then setting cold hands on her neck. "Be still," he warned coldly. "You'll blow us both up."

Allie's heart spluttered as the full realization of her situation took shape. Her attacker had fastened something large and heavy around her neck. Cold and hard like metal, the device forced her chin into an uncomfortable angle at the front.

He'd fitted her with a bomb collar.

Allie's chest tightened and her stomach rolled. She'd learned all about bombs like these while married to Max. Had read about the victims but couldn't recall any survivors. "Why are you doing this?" she whispered. "Please, just let me go."

"Shut. Up," he snarled. "Open your mouth again, and I'll detonate the bomb I left with your baby."

Allie's mouth snapped shut. Her parched tongue seemed to swell behind her teeth. And her limbs began to shake.

O'Lear leaned away and smiled. The dim light of a caged overhead bulb cast long shadows over his maniacal expression. "Now sit up." He grabbed her shoulder before she could obey and hoisted her roughly into a seated position. He jammed her back against a row of boxes along the wall. The tile where she'd been lying was stained with blood from her swollen lip, and probably her head where he'd knocked her unconscious.

She scanned the room with squinted eyes, fighting nausea as he fumbled for his phone. He was likely planning to taunt Max and the team with a text or photo. To flaunt his insanity. His deranged idea of superiority.

But a picture isn't a bad thing, she realized, shreds of hope floating in her battered, aching head. A photo was her chance to send the team a message. Opaline would find the clue, if Allie could leave one.

O'Lear tapped his phone screen, presumably writing his message.

Allie had seconds at the most to come up with a plan.

Think, she willed herself. It wasn't time to give in to the pain. Right now, she needed clarity. A way to alert the TCD to her location.

There were rows of cleaning materials on the shelves across from her, but nothing to suggest where she was. A pile of boxes pressed against her back, but she didn't dare attempt a look. She couldn't move. Couldn't risk drawing O'Lear's attention or somehow detonating the bomb.

O'Lear stepped back with a snarl, glaring at his phone. His heel crushed a small empty box, and he kicked it aside. The logo on the address label sent a jolt through her core.

Great Lakes Mall.

If the boxes behind her had the same label, there was still hope for Allie.

She pulled her arms in front of her, curving her shoulders and making herself as small as possible.

Attempting to give the best view possible of the boxes at her back.

When O'Lear raised the phone in front of him, eager to snap a photo of his battered, bomb-clad hostage, she wilted forward and to the side. She did her best to appear as injured as she felt, as if she couldn't possibly remain upright any longer, even while seated on the floor. A flash of light drew her haggard gaze up to meet his.

"Now he'll see," O'Lear said, tapping the screen with a sinister grin and palpable energy. "Now he'll know. I'm in charge here. And he's going to regret he ever provoked me."

And Allie hoped he was right on the first point. She hoped Max would see.

MAX PACED THE sidewalk outside the mall. Anger replaced the fear he'd felt all day while worrying for Allie's safety. Now he knew. He'd been right to worry. His initial bout of self-loathing had morphed quickly into primal rage as he'd waited, helpless, unable to save her. Not knowing where to begin.

He imagined the scene on repeat in his mind. Saw O'Lear breaking into Allie's home and overpowering her. Hitting her until she bled on her bedroom carpet. Had she been napping? Changing clothes? Had she heard him enter, then run to her room to hide?

Now she could be anywhere.

She could be dead.

Max pressed the heels of his hands against his

eyes, forcing the thought away. If Allie was gone. If Max was too late. There would be hell to pay for Fritz O'Lear, all consequences be damned. Because when Max got his hands on O'Lear—*when*, not *if*—he was going to tear him apart.

Thankfully, Allie's parents and Max Jr. had been taken into protective custody. He didn't have to worry for his son or in-laws. He could concentrate on O'Lear and Allie, as soon as he had something to work with. Until then, he was in a holding pattern. Simmering with fear and rage. Biding his time until someone told him where to find the criminal who'd dared lay a hand on Max's ex-wife.

Around him, his teammates made phone calls and chattered among themselves. Carly called Opaline to check her progress on finding O'Lear. Rihanna spoke privately with local news channels, requesting they scan the crowd and nearby area for signs of the bomber or his Toyota. Axel contacted Pamela, determined to get an idea of where the psychopath might've taken a hostage. He also asked the officer looking after her to use her phone to text Fritz, asking for a callback, but he didn't hold out much hope they'd get an answer, now that the man knew her phone was compromised.

Aria and Selena were meeting with the Grand Rapids bomb squad and a team of handlers and bomb-sniffing dogs on Max's behalf. Reviewing mall blueprints and relaying the plan Max had outlined for their search. Whatever was happening with Allie, the mall still needed to be searched. If there was a ticking bomb meant for Emilio West, the device still needed to be disarmed and recovered.

Max had removed himself from the mission. He couldn't do the job with his heart and head so inextricably tied to thoughts of Allie's abduction.

A sharp whistle turned him toward the group of hardworking TCD teammates, and he broke into a jog to reach them. It was the first they'd called for him since he'd walked away to pull himself together several minutes before, and he knew they wouldn't have intruded without a substantial lead.

"You have something?" he called, as his friend waved him close.

"Opaline was able to manipulate the photo of Allie." Axel passed his phone to Max. "We have confirmation on her location at the time the photograph was taken."

Max stared at the enhanced image on Axel's phone screen and felt the snap of purpose in his limbs.

The barely visible address label on a box against the wall behind her bore a familiar logo.

Great Lakes Mall.

ALLIE DRIFTED IN and out of consciousness, nauseated and dizzy with pain. She'd tipped back over, sliding down the collection of boxes to press her burning cheek and body against the cool tile floor. Her head spun and her stomach churned. Bile pooled in her mouth and sweat broke across her forehead.

Her thoughts wound over sweet, distant memories and through the more recent hell she'd lived today.

A round of footsteps tugged at her mind, piercing the hazy thoughts and bringing her back to the moment once more. She pressed her eyelids closed and her lips together tightly, praying Fritz O'Lear would just leave her alone. She couldn't run. Couldn't hide. Couldn't fight. What was left for him to do to her?

Besides press the button and blow her up.

Curiosity peeled her dry, itchy eyelids open to half-mast, and she was surprised by the darkness of the room. The overhead light had been extinguished, leaving only a faint red glow across the floor before her. A countdown, she presumed, from the bomb fixed around her neck.

Tears welled and slid over Allie's cheeks. She was both desperately thankful her parents had agreed to take Max Jr. for the day, and hopeful that O'Lear had kept his word not to hurt them.

At least this way, Max Jr. hadn't been home when O'Lear had broken in. Her baby hadn't been injured by the lunatic, or worse. He wasn't in jeopardy, and he hadn't witnessed his mother's abduction. All things she couldn't have protected him from.

She'd likely be dead soon, but at least her cooperation had saved her son.

Her breath caught, mid hazy thought. Whoever had been approaching stopped outside the closed door across from her. There was a strange snuffling. A heavy, breathy huffing. She blinked gritty eyes, sure it was a hallucination. The sound wasn't human.

It was animalistic and wild. The noises scratched at her consciousness, but her eyes fell shut again. The nausea was back, and pulling her under once more.

THE BOMB-SNIFFING canines and their handlers stopped before a brown metal door in a long corridor beneath the mall. The dogs sat, and the men turned to Max, tipping their heads and first two fingers toward the barrier.

Max motioned the men and canines back, then reached carefully for the doorknob, twisting the cool metal with his left hand and a silent prayer. He raised his sidearm in his right hand, ready to fire as needed, and hoping it wouldn't come to that in proximity with a bomb.

He swung the door open slowly, on high alert, as a wedge of light spread across the closet floor. A familiar form appeared on the ground across from him.

"Allie!" Max rushed to his ex-wife's side and fell to his knees on the tile. She was pale and bleeding, sweating and shaking. The collar bomb around her throat gave him only twelve minutes to set her free, and time was ticking.

A team of men and women, along with three canines, waited in the hall, lingering at the doorway. Dog handlers, bomb-squad members and Axel. Max had grabbed them all as he'd torn into the mall with one thing on his mind. Finding Allie.

Now here she was, with small red numbers counting down beneath her chin, and none of them were safe if Max screwed up.

"Get back!" Max yelled. "Retreat. I've got her. Everyone out!"

He didn't turn to watch them leave. The sounds of jogging feet and the rhythmic click of canine toe-nails told the story as they faded into the distance.

Max held Allie's cold tear- and blood-streaked face between his palms. "I've got you," he whispered, taking a closer look at the device beneath her chin.

A small digital clock had been attached to a galvanized pipe. The steel was bent into a circle around her neck. An imperfect device, and an obvious rush job in comparison to the precision designs of O'Lear's pressure cookers. He'd created this bomb in anger instead of reverence. And the haste had likely made the device far less stable.

Allie's eyes opened by small slits. Her swollen lip quivered, but her body remained eerily still.

"What can I do?" Axel asked, his voice booming in the dim, silent space.

Max started, twisting for a look over his shoulder at the man who'd been with him through every manner of danger and challenge. A man clearly too stupid to leave so he wouldn't be blown up. "What are you doing here?" Max scolded. "This bomb is unstable. Get back. Go with the others."

"Not a chance," Axel said. "I'm not leaving, and you don't have time to argue, so you might as well tell me what I can do."

Max wavered, torn between saving Axel's life and improving the odds of saving Allie. It was dark, and Max couldn't hold a light and work on the bomb. Plus, Axel was right. Every second spent arguing was a moment lost to the countdown. "Hold a flashlight over here."

Max didn't dare touch the switch on the wall. He couldn't trust it or anything else in this room not to blow them up. At less than ten minutes to go now, he'd have to make do with the tools on the utility vest he'd strapped on. Axel had insisted he wear a bomb vest beneath the tools, but they both knew the added protection was more of a talisman than protection. Nothing could save their lives at this range. Max was doubly thankful he hadn't taken the time to dress in a proper EOD suit before entering the facility. Time would have run out before he geared up, then slogged through the mall, down maintenance stairs and along the subterranean corridor to Allie.

A beam of light hit her pale face and she whimpered.

Axel swore.

Max knew the feeling. Allie's blood was visible everywhere beneath the light. On the floor and smeared across boxes, saturating the hair at the back of her head. She wasn't opening her eyes or speaking, probably because she couldn't. These kinds of injuries. This much blood. She was likely concussed. Probably weak, dizzy and nauseated. It was a miracle she was conscious. "I'm going to sit you up slowly," he explained. "I want to get a look at the entire device."

Max tilted her upright, then slightly forward, pushing hanks of sweaty and blood-soaked hair away from her back and shoulders. The sweet blond curls he loved were stuck to her skin and shirt. Max's eyes blurred with emotion. Seeing her like this was enough to undo him. "Okay," he said, satisfied there was nothing else to see. "I'm going to lay you down now."

"Go," she whimpered, tears falling from her eyes as Max lowered her to the floor. "Protect our baby. There's a bomb with him and my parents."

Max stilled. He glanced at Axel for confirmation. Axel shook his head. Negative.

"There's no bomb," Max told her. "Max Jr. and your parents are with the police. They're safe."

Allie's chest quaked, and a cry broke free. "I didn't fight because he told me…" She trailed off, sobs replacing words, and Max felt bile rise in his throat. O'Lear had threatened her family, and Allie had bent to his will.

Max settled her on her back, then caressed her cheeks with the pads of his thumbs. "You're going to be okay, too, baby. I will never leave you. And neither of us are dying here today."

He tipped her head against the tile, using extreme care. "Axel."

His partner moved into position beside him, crouching to focus the light so Max could work.

Allie's hand dragged across the floor, seeking and finding Max's knee. "I'm so sorry I believed him."

"This isn't your fault," Max assured her. "You couldn't take the risk. I would've done the same thing if I thought you or Max Jr. was in danger." He pulled a small screwdriver from his vest and removed the bottom panel from the clock.

"That can't be good," Axel whispered.

"Nope." Max stared at the tangle of wires and liberal use of putty. There were visible gaps between the metal and the clock from this viewpoint. Sloppy. Amateur. Reckless work. A visual representation of O'Lear's limited time and skills.

"What's the verdict?" Axel asked.

"Not good." The collar bomb was clearly as unstable as its maker. "There's no pressure. The blast will barely escape this room if it detonates. But it would destroy all the lives in it."

Axel nodded. "Then you'd better stop it before it goes off."

Max turned back to the wires, sorting and logging them quickly and mentally. "He doesn't want to kill me right now. He wants to punish me. Make me fail in my attempt to save her. But there's a flaw in his plan. I will never let that happen."

"No?" an unfamiliar voice asked.

Max and Axel jerked around, hands on guns. Stalling at the sight of Fritz O'Lear with a makeshift detonation device in his grip.

"You didn't think I'd leave again, did you?" O'Lear

asked. "The last time I set a bomb and left, you went rushing in and took it away."

"I'm not going anywhere without her," Max said. "So your plan is cracked. And you aren't leaving this building without handcuffs or being in an ambulance."

O'Lear smiled. He wasn't much to look at up close. Five foot ten, 180 pounds of dough. Unkempt beard, disheveled hair. He looked wild and childish, a grown man throwing a fit. Demanding respect instead of earning it.

What he needed was a time-out. Preferably in a federal prison with a lifetime of therapy. But that would come later. After Allie was safe.

Max turned his attention back to the bomb. Done wasting precious seconds on a psychopath.

"Stop!" O'Lear growled. "Get away from her."

Max ignored him. There were six minutes on the bomb. Six minutes left in Allie's life. He had to work fast.

"You should be grateful," O'Lear said, inching into the room. "You think you're doing the right thing. Being the hero. But she dumped you. She vowed to be with you forever. Richer and poorer. Good times and bad. But she left. She broke her promise." His voice grew louder with each new phrase, the words shaking from his tongue, as if he could barely contain the anger. "She humiliated you," he continued. "Tossed you aside, made you feel weak and pathetic, like you were an embarrassment. Like you were nothing. And she deserves payback."

"That was you," Max said. "Not me. None of this is about me. Or Allie." He ran his fingers along a set of thin wires connecting the clock and pipe. The space was small, his fingers broad, making it difficult to see and to work. "I love this woman," he said firmly. "I don't want to punish her. I want to save her." He patted his vest in search of the needle-nose pliers. If he could wiggle the wires out a bit, create some leeway in the tension, he might be able to disrupt the connection between the bomb and the detonator. Effectively removing O'Lear's power.

"Stop!" O'Lear screamed. "Stop touching her! She deserves punishment for what she did to you. And you deserve punishment for what you've done to me. You watch her die. Then I watch you die. You get the same thing they all get. Because I'm the one in control. Not you!"

"In five minutes, we all die," Max said. "Maybe you should start running."

"Hey, now," Axel said sharply, throwing his hands wide like an umpire. "I don't want to die. I'm just here on assignment. Someone told me to help this agent because a woman was in trouble." He turned his back to Max and Allie, leaving his light on the floor, pointed toward the bomb.

"What are you doing?" O'Lear asked.

"Pleading for my life," Axel said, lifting his palms and engaging the killer. "Please don't do this. I can understand why you want to. Women are spiteful and mean. But I want to live."

"This isn't about you," O'Lear sneered. "Shut. Up!"

"My girl broke my heart once," Axel continued. "She cheated. With my brother. And my best friend, Sarah."

O'Lear growled. "Women." He spit the word. "They make you feel good before they stab you in the heart. Men aren't any better. They all want to puff themselves up. Feel powerful, but they aren't."

"You are," Axel said. "You literally have power over our lives right now."

Max worked the tip of his small pliers under a pair of parallel wires, buried among the rest. Then he tugged slow and steady. Four minutes on the clock.

"What if you and I run?" Axel said. "There's still time. We can avoid the blast. Police will rush in, assume we're all dead, and we can get away."

"We won't get away," O'Lear said. "Not really, and not for long. There's no life for me out there now. That's why I've stayed. I'm finishing what I started."

Max's ears rang with that truth. It was a suicide mission all around. O'Lear had never intended to leave alive. He'd only wanted to spend his last few breaths knowing he was in control.

"I can't get Emilio. His bomb is still in the car. But I can get an FBI agent, and that's a good trade."

Max took a steadying breath and focused. Three minutes. He'd separated the most likely two wires to break the connection, but he didn't know which to cut. One wrong snip and they were dead.

"I came here with the police," Axel said, pressing on, apparently willing to distract O'Lear to his dying breath. "They pulled me off my shift for this. I can show you how to get out without being seen. You can start over. Maybe once things settle, you can come back and finish your work," he suggested. "Kill Pat and Emery."

"Pam and Emilio," O'Lear said. "And I'm not stupid. I know who you are. I've seen you on television with the others. You're FBI, he's FBI, and I'm in charge here."

Silence gonged through the room as O'Lear went still.

And Max understood. The timer had another two and a half minutes, but he was out of time. O'Lear never intended to let the timer reach zero. He had a detonator because he would decide when they died. He was in control. And control was all that mattered to him.

"Do it," Allie whispered, the sound calling him back to the wires at hand. Her pretty hazel eyes bored into him, tired and wary, but unafraid. She gripped his knee, squeezing where her fingers had rested through it all, a constant connection to him as he worked. "I trust you."

Max cut the yellow wire, following his gut as the familiar click of a detonator registered in the stillness behind him.

The red numbers on the clock disappeared.

And Axel lunged at the bomber.

Max ripped the clock and wires away from the

device, separating the explosives from a potential spark. He worked the metal pipe off Allie's neck with trained and certain hands, then swept her into his arms and headed for the hallway.

Axel and O'Lear stumbled and fought as Max slipped past them. It would only take seconds for Axel to bring the assailant into submission. No one was better at hand-to-hand combat than Axel.

"Max," Allie whispered. Her eyes rolled back, and she began to convulse.

"Allie?" Terror shrieked through him as his wife shook violently in his arms before going completely limp. "No! Allie! Stay with me," he pleaded.

The earsplitting boom of a discharged firearm ricocheted through the corridor a moment before Axel screamed, "Gun!"

Max dropped on instinct, squatting immediately and setting Allie on the floor. He twisted at the waist, gun drawn inside the next breath, and took aim at the scene behind him.

O'Lear raised his gun, and a second blast ran through the narrow space.

The bomber's gun toppled from his hand. He howled in pain as blood erupted from his thigh.

Max never missed a target. He scooped Allie's lifeless body back into his arms as Axel rolled the bomber onto his chest and cuffed him.

Then Max began to run.

Epilogue

Max led Allie into the elevator at TCD headquarters in Traverse City. It was a team tradition to celebrate with dinner after a job well done. It was also the first of these dinners that Allie had attended with Max since their original engagement, in the days before he'd begun to pull away. And he was humbled every moment by her willingness to join him tonight. Despite all he'd done wrong, Allie trusted him to change.

He wouldn't let her down.

She leaned into him and pressed a kiss against his lips as the elevator soared upward. "Have I thanked you for saving my life?" she asked sweetly, her small hands pressed to his chest.

"Once or twice," he said, gently kissing her back. "You know that without your quick thinking to make the mall's logo visible in O'Lear's photo, I wouldn't have found you in time." In Max's book, it was really Allie who'd saved her life. Her level head had made all the difference. And during questioning at the hospital, O'Lear had admitted to his plan of letting the clock reach zero if Max hadn't shown up. In that scenario, O'Lear would have beaten Max and left town victorious. But once Max had found her, and all the lawmen outside knew where they were, O'Lear had decided to use his backup plan. The detonator would allow him to maintain control. He'd die in the process, but it would be on his terms.

"How are you feeling?" Max asked, watching her expression for signs of bravado. "Your doctors said not to overdo it for a couple of weeks. It's only been one."

"I'm alive," she whispered, her gorgeous hazel eyes twinkling under the elevator's fluorescence. "I want to live. I can rest when we get home."

"One hour, tops," he said, skimming his fingers over the warm exposed skin along her collarbone. "Then I'm taking you home and getting you into bed."

She smiled. "If only that meant what I wish it meant."

"It means you need your rest," he said, pressing a kiss to her forehead.

Clingy black velvet covered her from wrists to waistline, hugging her perfect curves in delicious ways. A black-and-white floral pattern fell loosely over her hips and stopped at her knees. She was business casual, office chic, and as beautiful as any model or actress on the red carpet. Twice as smart and infinitely more desirable. In fact, there was no one else Max ever wanted on his arm again.

Too soon, the elevator stopped, and the doors parted.

Allie turned on simple flats, twining her fingers with his as they stepped onto the seventh-floor lobby.

The voices of Max's teammates and their guests rose above the din of clinking glasses, soft music and laughter.

"There they are," Alana called, crossing the space immediately to greet them with a warm smile. "You look stunning. Both of you," she said, dropping air-kisses near Allie's cheeks before squeezing Max's hand. "I'm so glad you're here. Come. Eat. Drink. Share."

"Thank you for putting the dinner off a few days," Max said. "This was the first night Allie has felt like herself." And he wouldn't have left her side if she hadn't been up to the trip.

"Yes, thank you," Allie agreed. "I really didn't want to miss it."

Alana smiled kindly in response. "We would've put this off as long as you needed. You're our guests of honor, after all."

The twinkle in the director's eye told Max she hadn't missed the presence of an engagement ring on Allie's finger. Or the reemergence of one, to be more accurate. To Max's complete delight, Allie had agreed to be his wife once more. They would be married in the spring, with their closest friends and family members at their sides. Afterward, Max had promised to take her anywhere she wanted to go, and Allie had requested a beach, someplace warm, without interruption. Her parents had cheerfully volunteered their babysitting services.

Aria and her fiancé, Grayson, were the next to approach. Each carrying a drink in both hands. Aria passed a glass of wine to Allie. Grayson handed Max a beer. "You made it," Aria said, attention fixed on Allie. "I guess the rumors are true. You are one tough cookie."

Allie laughed. "I try, but I probably shouldn't stay long." She accepted the drink, then offered Grayson her hand. "I'm Allie McRay. I had the pleasure of meeting your fiancée last week when she and this team saved my life."

"Grayson," he said, accepting the shake. "This team has saved me, too. In more ways than one," he said, shooting a tender look at his date.

Max wound a protective arm around Allie's waist, fighting the flash of memory that always accompanied the subject of Fritz O'Lear. Allie had been lucky to escape with her life.

Allie rested her head against his shoulder, sensing his unease, or maybe feeling the same residual emotions herself. "I was lucky," she said. "Despite a homicidal serial bomber's best attempt, I made it home from the hospital with only a few stitches. No concussion, though Max and an EEG say I had a seizure. I don't remember that. The rest, I wish I could forget. But as long as I don't do too much at one time, I'm feeling remarkably well. I'm expecting a complete recovery."

"We're all very glad," Aria said.

Allie gazed up at Max. "I'm not ashamed to admit this is the first time I've worn anything but pajamas in a week. Though I can't say I've had cause to wear a dress in about two years. Being the mother of a toddler isn't as glamorous as you might think."

"You are preaching to the choir," Aria said, her smile going wide at the mention of her newest family member. "Our son, Danny, barely lets me brush my teeth these days." She hooked her arm through Grayson's. "But I wouldn't change a thing."

Max sipped his beer, enjoying the moment. He'd been given a second chance with Allie that he never thought he'd have, and he didn't want to miss a single one of her smiles.

"It gets easier." Allie laughed. "Eventually they sleep through the night, or so I'm told."

"What does?" Carly asked, sliding between Aria and Allie, with her fiancé, Noah, on her arm.

"Babies," Allie said.

Carly smiled, and Noah pulled her close. "Well, I'm glad you all found a sitter," she said. Her gaze trailed curiously over Max and Allie, then stopped at Allie's diamond ring. "What is this?" She lifted Allie's left hand in both of hers. "It's back!"

Allie laughed. "It is." She passed her wine to Max, so she could hug Carly with both arms.

He set the glass on a nearby table, happily enjoying the view. Allie was beautiful, fierce and so incredibly kind. He'd been a complete idiot for ever letting her go.

Opaline's laugh carried through the room, and Max turned to catch her eye. "Max!" She started in his direction, then adjusted her path slightly when she noticed Allie at his side. "Allie!" The women hugged, and Allie's eyes misted.

"I missed you," Allie confessed. "You look amazing. As always."

Opaline did a weird curtsy, then spun in her vintage pinup dress and heels. "Back at ya. I didn't expect to see you here. What are you? Superwoman?"

Allie sniffled and batted back tears. "I think that title already belongs to you."

A wolf whistle turned the group around, and Axel strode into view. His gaze jumped to Selena, still across the room, before pulling back to Allie. "Ms. McRay." He lifted her left hand to inspect the ring when he arrived. "You know it's not too late for us, right? I've got a car waiting outside."

"In your dreams," Max said, clapping his buddy warmly on the shoulder. He owed Axel everything. He couldn't have saved Allie on his own.

"How are you?" Axel asked, looking more serious as his gaze trailed over Allie's face, lingering on the barely masked split of her lip.

"I'm okay," she said. "All things considered. It's my first outing since we left the mall, unless you count leaving the hospital."

"I don't," he said. "But I'm glad you're here." Axel's gaze jumped to Selena as she made her way toward the group, and the muscle in his jaw ticked.

"Hello," Selena said, widening their circle by another half foot. She bit into her lip and looked away from Axel. "How's everyone doing?"

Max looked from Selena to Axel, wondering what he'd missed and hoping they hadn't slept together. Things would be inevitably awkward after that.

Allie studied the pair, as well, brows furrowed as she considered them. "Axel, I've been meaning to ask you. When you were distracting O'Lear from killing me, you told him women were the worst."

"Boo," Carly said. Aria scoffed, and Selena wrinkled her nose.

Axel raised his palms. "I was only trying to keep him busy. You all know I love women."

"Boo," Carly repeated. Aria laughed, but Selena still wrinkled her nose.

"You said you'd had your heart broken," Allie went on. "Was that true?"

Axel shrugged. "Sure. Everyone's had a heartbreak. Right?"

"I suppose," she agreed. "Are you seeing anyone now?"

"Hey," he said softly, "I was serious about that car waiting outside."

Max chuckled. "Watch it, Morrow."

"All right," Allie said. "At least tell me Fritz O'Lear is going to be punished for the lives he took."

Axel nodded. "That I can confirm. Alana and I worked with the Grand Rapids PD and the TCD to create an ironclad case against him. O'Lear will be held fully accountable for every crime he committed. His victims and their families will have justice."

Allie wrapped her arms around Max's middle and rested her head against his side. "Thank you. All of you," she said, dragging her attention to each member of Max's team.

Pride swelled in Max's chest, and he saw it reflected in his teammates' eyes.

Opaline raised her brows at Selena, and Selena looked away.

Hopefully, the sisters would work out their differences sooner rather than later. They were lucky to have one another, and the members of his team knew firsthand that no one was promised another day.

"Let's eat," Axel said, waving an arm toward the catered buffet behind them. "I'm starving."

The group slowly folded in on itself, breaking up slightly as they made their way toward the food.

Time to eat, drink and celebrate what they had. A large and growing family. One that Max was proud to see Allie become a real part of.

He pulled out a chair for her at the table, and she turned to kiss his cheek.

Her hands grazed his chest, looping lazily around the back of his neck and pulling him down to meet her. "I love you," she whispered. "Thank you for bringing me here tonight. And for finally letting me be part of your team."

Max released the chair in favor of circling her with his arms. "You are my team," he said and brushed a kiss against her ear.

* * * * *

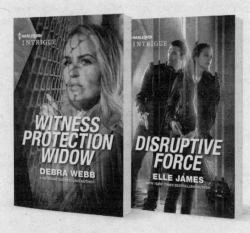

#1977 HUNTING A KILLER
Tactical Crime Division: Traverse City • by Nicole Helm
When K-9 handler Serena Lopez discovers her half brother's a fugitive from justice, she must find him—and his dangerous crew. It's a good thing her partner is lead agent Axel Morrow. But as cunning as the duo may be, it's a race against time to catch the criminals before they kill again.

#1978 PURSUIT OF THE TRUTH
West Investigations • by K.D. Richards
Security expert Ryan West's worst fears come to life when hotel CEO Nadia Shelton is nearly killed. Someone will do anything to find the brother Nadia thought was dead, and Ryan will have to stay strictly professional to protect her. But the sparks igniting between them are impossible to ignore.

#1979 HIDEOUT AT WHISKEY GULCH
The Outriders Series • by Elle James
After saving a woman and baby from would-be kidnappers, ex-marine Matt Hennessey must help Aubrey Blanchard search for the baby's abducted sister. Can they bring down a human trafficking cartel in the process?

#1980 THE WITNESS
A Marshal Law Novel • by Nichole Severn
Checking in on his witness in protective custody, marshal Finn Reed finds Camille Goodman fighting an attacker. Finn is determined to keep the strong-willed redhead alive, but soon a serial killer's twisted game is playing out—one that the deputy and his fearless witness may not survive.

#1981 A LOADED QUESTION
STEALTH: Shadow Team • by Danica Winters
When a sniper shoots at STEALTH contractor Troy Spade, he knows he must cooperate with the FBI. As Troy and Agent Kate Scot get closer to the truth, secrets from Kate's family will be revealed. How are they involved...and what are they willing to do to keep themselves safe?

#1982 COLD CASE COLORADO
An Unsolved Mystery Book • by Cassie Miles
Vanessa Whitman moves into her eccentric uncle's remote castle to ghostwrite his memoir, but then Sheriff Ty Coleman discovers a body in a locked room of the Colorado castle, transforming everyone in Vanessa's family into potential killers.

Prologue

The tears leaked out of Kay Duvall's eyes, even as she tried to
focus on what she had to do. *Had* to do to bring Ben home safe.

She fumbled with her ID and punched in the code that
would open the side door, usually only used for a guard taking a
smoke break. It would be easy for the men behind her to escape
from this side of the prison.

It went against everything she was supposed to do.
Everything she considered right and good.

A quiet sob escaped her lips. They had her son. How could
she not help them escape? Nothing mattered beyond her son's
life.

"Would you stop already?" one of the prisoners muttered.
He'd made her give him her gun, which he now jabbed into her
back. "Crying isn't going to change anything. So just shut up."

She didn't care so much about her own life or if she'd be
fired. She didn't care what happened to her as long as they let
her son go. So she swallowed down the sobs and blinked out as
many tears as she could, hoping to stem the tide of them.

She got the door open and slid out first—because the man holding the gun pushed it into her back until she moved forward.

They came through the door behind her, dressed in the clothes she'd stolen from the locker room and Lost and Found. Anything warm she could get her hands on to help them escape into the frigid February night.

Help them escape. Help three dangerous men escape prison. When she was supposed to keep them inside.

It didn't matter anymore. She just wanted them gone. If they were gone, they'd let her baby go. They had to let her baby go.

Kay forced her legs to move, one foot in front of the other, toward the gate she could unlock without setting off any alarms. She unlocked it, steadier this time if only because she kept thinking that once they were gone, she could get in contact with Ben.

She flung open the gate and gestured them out into the parking lot. "Stay out of the safety lights and no one should bug you."

"You better hope not," one of the men growled.

"The minute you sound that alarm, your kid is dead. You got it?" This one was the ringleader. The one who'd been in for murder. Who else would he kill out there in the world?

Guilt pooled in Kay's belly, but she had to ignore it. She had to live with it. Whatever guilt she felt would be survivable. Living without her son wouldn't be. Besides, she had to believe they'd be caught. They'd do something else terrible and be caught.

As long as her son was alive, she didn't care.

Don't miss
Hunting a Killer *by Nicole Helm,*
available February 2021 wherever
Harlequin Intrigue books and ebooks are sold.

Harlequin.com

Get 4 FREE REWARDS!

We'll send you 2 FREE Books plus 2 FREE Mystery Gifts.

Harlequin Intrigue books are action-packed stories that will keep you on the edge of your seat. Solve the crime and deliver justice at all costs.

FREE Value Over $20

YES! Please send me 2 FREE Harlequin Intrigue novels and my 2 FREE gifts (gifts are worth about $10 retail). After receiving them, if I don't wish to receive any more books, I can return the shipping statement marked "cancel." If I don't cancel, I will receive 6 brand-new novels every month and be billed just $4.99 each for the regular-print edition or $5.99 each for the larger-print edition in the U.S., or $5.74 each for the regular-print edition or $6.49 each for the larger-print edition in Canada. That's a savings of at least 12% off the cover price! It's quite a bargain! Shipping and handling is just 50¢ per book in the U.S. and $1.25 per book in Canada.* I understand that accepting the 2 free books and gifts places me under no obligation to buy anything. I can always return a shipment and cancel at any time. The free books and gifts are mine to keep no matter what I decide.

Choose one: ☐ **Harlequin Intrigue**   ☐ **Harlequin Intrigue**
             Regular-Print   **Larger-Print**
             (182/382 HDN GNXC)   (199/399 HDN GNXC)

Name (please print)

Address   Apt. #

City   State/Province   Zip/Postal Code

Email: Please check this box ☐ if you would like to receive newsletters and promotional emails from Harlequin Enterprises ULC and its affiliates. You can unsubscribe anytime.

> ### Mail to the **Reader Service:**
> **IN U.S.A.:** P.O. Box 1341, Buffalo, NY 14240-8531
> **IN CANADA:** P.O. Box 603, Fort Erie, Ontario L2A 5X3

Want to try 2 free books from another series! Call **1-800-873-8635** or visit www.ReaderService.com.